HUMAN OF FLESH

JAMES FERRENTINO

ISBN: 979-8-218-93824-6

Every shot felt useless.

But I kept firing anyway, just to make the noise. Just to pretend I mattered. I reloaded with shaking hands, biting back curses as powder spilled, as the ramrod slipped, as my fingers refused to obey.

I clutched the gun like it was the last honest thing left in the world.

I gathered whatever energy I had.

I rose again.

BAM.

The bullet tore through my right shoulder like a saw.

At first, I didn't understand what had happened, only that heat had suddenly appeared inside the cold. Then the sting became a burn, and the burn became a blooming pain that stole my breath.

My knees folded.

I hit the ground hard enough to knock the air out of me, and blood pulsed with my heartbeat, spreading into the snow in dark, steaming bursts.

The world narrowed.

Noise softened. Shouting turned far away. The cold stopped arguing with my skin.

And then… peace.

Comfort washed over me as my blood spilled out. For the first time in weeks, I felt warm. Not truly warm, but released. The pain was strange, distant, almost gentle compared to the long misery that came before it.

My eyelids grew heavy.

I let them.

I shut my eyes.

Blackness.

Chapter Two
BURIED

I swung my arms wide.

My children ran to me, laughing, and my wife followed, bright in the sun, her dress whispering in the wind. The world was warm and whole.

Then her arms closed around us.

Warmth flooded me.

Her embrace tightened.

Too tight.

My ribs compressed. My lungs couldn't rise. The sky dimmed. The wind died. My family blurred and vanished like smoke.

I woke.

Darkness.

Dirt pressed against my lashes. Grit packed my mouth. My ears felt stuffed with soil until even my heartbeat sounded far away.

I was buried alive.

I tried to move.

Nothing.

My legs were pinned. My left arm might as well have been nailed to my ribs. My chest barely twitched, stealing air in tiny, humiliating sips.

The terror wasn't the dirt.

It was the air.

I tried to breathe deeper. Dust slid down my throat. I gagged, choking on earth like it was water.

Move. MOVE.

I fought once and stole what little air I had left.

Then I heard it.

Digging.

A steady scrape overhead. Metal biting stone. Each strike traveled through my bones.

Someone was up there.

Voices filtered down, muffled but close.

"Bones," one said. "Human, I think."

"There's something else," another voice. "Some kind of old weapon."

A pause.

"A… musket?"

The word landed strangely.

Why would a man hesitate over that?

The voices drifted away.

And then I discovered my right arm could move.

Just a little.

I scraped dirt beside my ribs. Again. Again. Packed tight.

My fingertips broke into emptiness.

A pocket of air.

Not enough to live in.

Enough to know what living felt like.

I took the smallest breath I'd ever taken and it still tasted like dirt.

Then the ground split.

A wet crack. Dirt collapsed onto my face and chest. Light speared in, blinding and invasive. Cold air punched down into my grave.

I coughed mud and clawed forward, dragging myself through the opening as the earth slumped and clung.

And then…

I was out.

Sprawled. Exposed. Shivering beneath a sky I didn't recognize, with the certainty that I had crossed a boundary I was never meant to return from.

There was no battle. No smoke. No shouting.

Just a clearing shaved down to mud.

Huge yellow machines crouched nearby, iron beasts with claws and giant shovels, chewing the earth.

In the distance, a door opened on a massive metal carriage, a box on wheels. A person climbed down in bright, unfamiliar clothes.

Then the light caught them.

Their skin flashed gold, faintly glowing as if lit from beneath.

My stomach went cold.

Not men, my mind decided.

Something wearing men. Monsters.

I ducked back into the trench, stayed low, and pressed into shadow.

Their voices shifted away.

Just far enough.

I dropped into a prone position and I crawled. Inches at a time.

There was a small forest just about twenty feet away. There, I must take refuge.

I dragged myself into the brush and let it swallow me.

Only when my grave was out of sight did I collapse against a thin tree, bark cold beneath my fingers.

I stayed there, motionless. Catching my breath and regaining my nerve.

And in the faint light under the trees, I saw what clung to my skin.

A dusting of green.

Fine as ash, glowing like crushed emerald.

It pulsed once. Like magic.

Slow.

Living.

Chapter Three
IDENTIFY

Night fell, but it did not bring darkness.

The sky faded to a pale, washed blue, as if someone had forgotten to finish the day. The sun slipped below the horizon and the light simply stayed. Stars should have followed. Instead there were only one or two bright points, like pins pressed through cloth.

Everything looked strange in that half-light.

The trees around me seemed thin and frail. Narrow trunks, sparse branches, leaves that barely stirred even when the air moved. They didn't shelter. They watched. The forest felt shallow, like a sketch of itself.

I built a fire to steady my hands.

Not because I was cold. The air held no bite. But the flicker of flame was something that soothed me. I gathered deadwood, snapped it, struck sparks until the fire took. It burned clean and bright, casting light that barely fought the sky's pale glow.

I sat close anyway.

The quiet pressed in from every side. There were no insects nor distant animals. Not even wind. Just stillness. Heavy and listening, like the world was holding its breath.

I stared into the flame and waited for something to feel right.

Nothing did.

The fire snapped and settled, a sound that lived deep in my memory. The sound of fire serenaded my fondest moments. A sound that used to mean safety, warmth, friendship, and love.

I let it pull at me.

Then it answered something.

A second snapping, out of rhythm with the flames. Evenly spaced. Too deliberate.

From the distance.

Crunching.

Aggressive. Fast. Closing.

Instinct took over. I reached for my knife.

My pocket was gone.

So was the knife.

The crunching hit again, louder now, paired with a low vibration. Something heavy forcing its way through undergrowth without caring what it broke.

Whatever it was, it wasn't wandering.

It was coming straight for me.

The steps had the cadence of an animal, but they were too even. Too rhythmic. Too perfect.

My stomach tightened.

I rose, lunged three steps and a hop, and dropped low behind brush, kneeling, breath locked in my throat.

The sound cut through the trees in a straight line, like it already knew where I was. Branches bent. Leaves whispered. The approach never faltered.

The fire crackled beside me, suddenly too loud. A foolish beacon I couldn't undo.

Then the approaching creature broke through the brush and stopped.

Firelight caught metal.

Four legs. Plated armor. A dog's shape, but strange, with a shell not from nature. Between overlapping seams, ember-orange light pulsed faintly, like heat trapped beneath a skin that wasn't skin. In the center of its head sat a single round eye, lit blue.

It angled its head toward the fire.

The flame died.

Not sputtered. Not smothered.

Gone.

Like blowing out a candle.

Heat vanished with it, like the night had swallowed the last proof I was alive.

Darkness snapped into place.

Only weeds and thin brush separated us. I stayed frozen, knowing movement would be confession.

The blue eye turned.

Found me.

The iron dog advanced, crushing earth with the weight of a horse despite its smaller body. Each step sent a faint tremor through the ground, up through my knees.

I eased back inch by inch, careful not to wake a leaf.

It pushed through the weeds, stopped, and stared straight into me.

Then a light ignited.

Instant. White.

My vision vanished in one violent blink. My eyes screamed. I cried out and threw my arm up, burying my face against where my sleeve should have been.

The light didn't waver.

Unmoving. Patient.

My heartbeat roared in my ears.

Then a voice spoke. Flat and close, as if the word had been thrown like a spear.

"IDENTIFY."

I forced my eyes open a fraction, blinking through tears. Shapes bled back in around the edges of the light.

I swallowed grit.

"Private Gregory," I said, voice raw. "Continental Army. North Jersey."

The words felt ridiculous the moment they left my mouth.

I had just identified myself to a dog.

"Warning," it barked. "Stop where you are. You have broken curfew. Authorities have been alerted. Kneel on the ground."

I took one step back.

The dog reacted like a trigger being pulled.

Blue light snapped outward in a tight lattice. Cold lightning weaving around my chest, my arms, my legs. The moment it touched, my muscles turned to stone.

My body locked.

Even the effort to resist felt delayed, like my will had to travel through syrup to reach my hands.

I toppled over like a broom and hit the ground hard, frozen in place, staring up at weeds while the blue web zapped and surged, holding me like an insect pinned under glass.

The sky answered.

A thunderous note, low and musical, like a piano key struck too hard.

The air changed. Pressure pressed into my ears. My teeth chattered from the vibration.

Something huge appeared above the trees.

At first it looked like a cannonball. Dark and round against the pale-blue sky. It descended with slow, perfect patience.

It stopped over the treetops.

I braced for impact.

It didn't fall.

The forest beneath it reacted before my mind could. Leaves quivered. Branches shivered. Then the trees directly under its shadow vanished.

Gone.

At the sound of barely a crack, what remained were a few falling needles and rogue leaves.

Just absence. Clean and surgical. A wound cut into the world.

The sphere lowered again, steady and calm, never touching the earth. It hovered a foot above the soil, like an infant raising their feet to grass.

The top twisted like a lid being unscrewed.

A seam appeared.

A hatch split open.

A ramp unfolded with a soft mechanical groan.

Two men stepped out.

They wore shining armor like knights. Mirror-bright, hard as iron. Thin seams along their suits glowed with a subtle orange pulse, like a slow heartbeat. Their helmets were smooth and featureless. Nothing to read.

They moved down the ramp with quiet confidence.

Each carried a weapon that did not belong in any century I knew. It wasn't shaped for smoke or recoil. It looked more like an accessory.

They approached in perfect step and stopped.

Right over me.

The blue lightning still held me down. My muscles twitched uselessly. I could not lift a hand. Could not roll away.

Only my eyes moved.

I looked up at them, and for the first time since the bullet tore through my shoulder, I felt something worse than pain.

Powerless.

One of the men spoke.

"God damn," he said, like a habit, like a word that meant nothing.

"What is that?" he added. "It looks like a zombie."

Fear flared.

Then something hotter took its place.

Anger.

How dare he throw the Lord's name into the dirt like that.

My mind snapped for a shape that could hold the horror.

Devils. Demons. If hell wasn't fire, then it was this. A clean world with clean machines that erased trees without touching them.

The blue lattice cut out like a switch.

My limbs came back all at once.

I lurched up and shouted, "Satan, get back!"

The men stared at each other.

One laughed. Short, confused.

"Satan?" he repeated. "What is that?"

Then they were on me.

A hand clamped my arm like an iron vise. The second took the other side.

I fought. Kicking, twisting, prayers spilling out of me like breath in winter.

It did nothing.

They dragged me toward the hovering sphere as if I weighed nothing. My toes dug into dirt. My knees scraped. I was hauled up the ramp, half-carrying, half-sliding, my prayers turning frantic, useless in a God-forsaken place.

Inside, they threw me into a seat.

Blue lightning snapped around me again. My body went rigid, pinned upright.

The two men sat across from me, calm as if this was ordinary. They set their weapons down. Strapped themselves in.

The hatch sealed shut without a sound.

One of them pressed something on the wall. The lights dimmed.

I waited for motion. The lurch of travel, the shake of wheels, the pull of flight.

Nothing moved.

No acceleration. No sensation.

Only silence.

Chapter Four
NEW YORK

It felt like an hour. Maybe more. Time had no edges in that chamber, only breath and silence and the steady lie of stillness.

Then the hatch opened.

And beyond it was an entirely different place.

My stomach dropped.

I hadn't felt movement. Not a sway, not a turn, not even the faint lift of ascent. Nothing a man could cling to as proof he'd been carried anywhere at all.

Yet the door didn't open back onto the forest.

It opened onto another world.

Warm air hit my face, carrying a scent I couldn't name. Not smoke. Not earth. Something washed of all life. Clinical, yet humid like steam.

The blue lightning released me.

My limbs came back.

They seized my arms again.

By then I understood the truth. Fighting was useless. I didn't follow because I agreed. I followed because there was nothing else I could do.

They marched me down the ramp, the knights' steps ringing metal on metal as we crossed the threshold. Then the sound spilled into open space and vanished, like sound could not find its way back.

We stepped onto a wide platform suspended high above the earth.

And the world fell away.

Below stretched a city so vast my mind refused it at first. An engineered empire. Layered terraces descending into distance, carved with paths that moved like veins through stone. Buildings rose in clean rounded shapes, defying geometry, as if the city had been poured and allowed to harden.

Far below, figures moved through it, countless and small, swallowed by scale.

Ahead, towers climbed like castles, but they were not stone. They were iron and glass. Smooth glass with no waves nor ripples. Perfectly clear of defect. Bands of light ran along their faces in slow pulses, climbing and sinking like living snakes.

No candles burned here.

The light did not flicker. It held steady in hues I had no names for. It spilled from seams, traced the ground in thin ribbons, guided paths that curved through the city like drawn lines on a map.

And the sky.

The sky was not empty.

Iron birds cut through the pale-blue night. Some left blue flame behind them, clean strokes across the air. Others moved in coordinated clusters, silent as thought, darting between towers and vanishing behind glass only to reappear higher.

My mind tried to name them. Hawks. Crows. Cannon shot.

None fit.

These were not living things. They were machines that flew like they had always owned the air.

The guards holding my arms looked up too.

For the first time, their posture shifted. Subtle. A tightening of shoulders. A slight tilt of their featureless helmets.

Concern.

Not for me.

For the sky.

Above, the iron birds changed formation. Several banked hard toward something distant. The blue trails bent like brushstrokes across the night. The city's lights dimmed a fraction, then steadied again, like a heartbeat that had stumbled and recovered.

I stood on that platform with two strangers gripping my arms, a city of iron and light beneath my feet, and a sky full of metal wings above my head.

Ahead stood a door, the largest I had ever seen. Not wood. Not stone. Polished metal, smooth as glass and dark as iron, shining with a cold reflection that made my skin crawl.

I was face to face with someone I did not recognize.

This was the first time since I left for war that I saw my own face. I looked like a shadow that had learned to wear a man.

Mud crusted my forehead. Soil smeared my cheeks, dark and glittering green, packed under my nails, ground into my pores. My eyes sat too bright in a face too hollow. Cheeks sunk. A thinness that wasn't youth, but loss.

The uniform hanging off me was more rag than coat, stretched over bone, darkened by earth and time.

I should have seen a wound.

I should have seen the ruin of my right shoulder. Proof of the moment I fell.

But when I turned, angling toward the reflection, there was nothing.

No wound. No scar. Not even a trace.

My shoulder was whole, unmarked, as if the bullet had never found me at all.

Cold spread through my ribs, quick and sick.

We walked toward the door.

What was left of my boots flopped and squeaked against the platform. Every step sounded so clear, without an echo, lost in the vastness. The city behind me breathed with rouge gusts of wind, the air felt thick.

Waiting for the door to open.

I drew in a deep breath.

Before my lungs were even half full, two violent cracks tore through the sky.

Sharp, metallic snaps, like the world itself had been struck with a hammer.

The two spears of light dropped from above and hit the two men at my sides.

It split them clean in half at the waist, as if an invisible blade had fallen through them with perfect precision.

I snapped my gaze to my own waist and clawed at my skin, panic surging. Nothing. I wasn't hit.

Their legs took one last step while their upper bodies pitched backward in unison. They hit the platform with a hard clatter.

There was no blood.

Their torsos looked like uprooted trees. With a spray of sparks. Wires reaching in different directions. And oil of blue and orange slowly dripping forming a puddle of gray.

My stomach dropped so hard it felt like I had fallen through the platform.

I stumbled back and hit the ground, palms scraping metal, staring at what my mind refused to name.

Their upper halves still moved.

One helmet turned toward me in a slow, stunned motion, as if even it could not understand what had happened. A hand twitched, fingers flexing at air. The other tried to lift its weapon, dragging it uselessly, as if obeying some dying command.

Their voices erupted at once, sharp and frantic, the calm finally gone.

"We're under attack!"

"Council, respond!"

The words crashed over me and something colder than fear slid into place.

They were not men.

They were machines dressed like knights. Machines that spoke like soldiers. Machines that pretended to be human well enough to curse heaven and hell.

And now something in this world wanted them dead.

For the first time in a long time, my body snapped into motion without hesitation.

I did not pray.

I did not think.

I ran.

I sprinted down the metal ramp, away from the great doors, while the iron birds above circled and screamed through the sky.

They fired beams and bursts of light at the towering castle. In answer, more knights poured from the doors and ran to stations along the walls, raising strange weapons that threw bright lines back into the air.

This was no musket fight.

This was a battle in the heavens.

I took the slanted plank to a lower platform, then another, then another, dropping fast toward the streets below. My legs shook with every step, not from weakness, but because my mind could not keep up with the world.

When I finally hit the ground, I stopped for half a second.

The street smooth and seamless, a dark surface that shone under the city's light like a pond.

My shoes were nearly ruined. The leather on my soles had worn thin, and each step scraped like a knife.

I kicked my boots off, and I ran.

People flooded the streets, but they looked different. Their clothes clung tight and clean, like a second skin. Nothing I could name. And their faces glowed with the now familiar soft golden pulse.

And when they saw me, they screamed.

Not at the sky. Not at the burning towers. Not at the iron birds raining light.

At me.

Some were already running from the battle. But the moment they caught sight of my torn uniform and dirt-caked face, their panic doubled. They recoiled as if I carried a plague. They pointed. They shouted words I couldn't catch.

"They're here!" a voice screamed. "A flesh one!"

Heads whipped. People recoiled. And then they surged.

I shoved through, weaving between bodies, down streets lit by strange colors and endless glowing signs that hurt my eyes.

I looked for something natural.

Grass. A tree. A patch of earth.

There was nothing.

Only iron and glass and light, like the world had been scrubbed of anything that could rot.

My instinct told me to keep moving, so I did.

I passed a window where bright drinks glowed behind glass like jewels. Another where books hovered in the air, floating above a display as if held by invisible hands. The covers were clear like ice. The pages shimmered.

Then the sky struck.

Light slammed into the street ahead and detonated into heat and sparks. The shopfront exploded in a shower of glass and smoke. The shockwave slapped my face with glass and rubble. People screamed again and were instantly silenced by the dust billowing down the street like a flash flood.

I flinched and lunged into the nearest doorway.

Inside were racks of strange clothing, all smooth lines and dark colors, meant for bodies that had never marched through snow or bled into dirt. I tore off my rags and grabbed the first thing my hands found, a one-piece suit of dark fabric that looked a little big but about my size.

I jumped into it punching all of my limbs into sleeves.

I searched for buttons. Ties. Anything familiar.

There was nothing.

But then, to my surprise, the suit sealed itself, and shrunk down to my size, with a soft click, like it knew where I ended and it began.

I felt less exposed and protected. Taking deep breaths of clean air and trying to catch my breath, I felt a mixture of sweat and blood dripping down my face. I wiped my brow with my sleeve, feeling the splinters of glass embedded in my face.

Then another crack split the air outside and the building trembled.

I ran again.

The attacks intensified.

Beams of lightning carved down. Bursts of light shattered walls. The city flashed and flared around me as if the sky was trying to erase it one street at a time.

I turned down a narrow alley where fewer people ran, where shadow held longer. I chased silence like it could hide me.

Then a hand caught my arm.

I whipped around, ready to strike.

But the pull was not violent.

It was urgent. Careful.

The hand yanked me into a doorway just as light flared across the alley mouth. The door slammed shut, and the world outside vanished.

Warmth.

Dim lighting.

Quiet.

An old man stood inches from me, his beard long, his face lined and calm in a way nothing else in this city had been.

He pressed a finger to his lips.

"Quiet," he whispered. "You're safe here. I'm Elit."

I stared at him, lungs burning. "What made you take me in?"

He didn't answer.

He stood near the door, listening, as if the building itself might betray us. A distant impact rolled through the walls. Not close. Close enough.

He wore a face of calculation.

Then his gaze dropped.

Not to my clothes.

To my hands.

The faint green shimmer clung to my skin, catching the light when I moved.

Elit crouched slowly, as if approaching something volatile.

"You didn't resist," he said.

"Resist what?"

His eyes tracked the glow, not my face. "That's why it worked."

My pulse kicked harder. "What worked?"

He rose again, careful now, like he'd realized how close he was standing.

"Most minds panic when the body fails," he said. "They fight the end. Tear themselves apart. And go to the white light."

He paused.

"You didn't."

I looked down and rubbed my thumb across my knuckles.

The green didn't smear.

Didn't flake.

It stayed.

Elit took a half step toward me without thinking, then stopped himself.

"If anyone else saw you like this…" he said quietly, "you'd be taken in minutes."

The word snagged in my chest. "Taken?"

"Yes."

Something in his tone made the word worse instead of better.

"Then you brought me here to help," I said.

For the first time, he looked directly at me.

"I brought you here so you wouldn't disappear."

Another tremor rippled through the walls. Somewhere above us, something screamed.

Elit didn't look up.

"I know what you are."

"I'm a man," I snapped. "What else would I be?"

His voice dropped.

"A Human of Flesh."

The words landed with weight, like a classification I hadn't consented to.

"I don't understand."

A new impact rattled the ceiling. Dust whispered down a seam.

Elit crossed to a narrow slit in the wall and checked the street outside. When he spoke again, it was quieter.

"You're not from this year," he said. "Not from this way of life."

"I'm not from this *place*, of course. But, what do you mean *year*?" I said. "I was fighting the British yesterday. There was snow in…I was buried alive. I don't know why… A place with trees that look ill and a night that wouldn't go dark… I can't think straight."

My heart raced and I struggled to catch my breath.

"And then some knights took me."

I hesitated. Then froze.

"…Is this hell?"

Elit let out a dry breath.

"I haven't heard that word in a long time."

"Then where am I?"

He studied me like a man deciding whether a bridge would hold.

"This is New York."

I shook my head. "No."

"It is," he said. "Just not the one you know."

My stomach turned.

"So, if I'm wrong, and you're not from the past, then please, tell me your story. Go ahead," he pressured.

"I was recruited to fight the British…," I froze. What I was saying just didn't sound right, nothing was adding up.

That did it.

Something shifted behind his eyes.

"Ah-hah. So you're telling me that you're a free agent now," he said softly. "Because your war is long over."

"I'm not," I snapped. "I was shot. Buried. I died."

He nodded once.

"But," he said, "you didn't die, as you are here now in the flesh. And the Revolutionary War is over. Congratulations, you did it. You won," Elit said while sarcastically clapping his hands.

"The United States of America became independent, and then a thousand years later, evolved into The Order of the Earth. As you saw so intimately out there." He pointed outside through the crack of a window.

"What year is it?"

He hesitated.

That hesitation felt like a blade sliding in.

"Three… five… five… two."

The room tilted.

"No," I said. "It can't be," the word tilted and spun beneath my feet. "It's 1776."

Elit stepped closer and lowered his voice until it barely existed.

"Now that you're above ground," he said, "you're the rarest thing left in this city."

Another distant crack shook the building.

"I think you can survive here," he added, eyes flicking upward, "if you understand what you are."

My pulse hammered. "Survive what?"

He looked at me differently now. Not with pity.

With assessment.

"I'm part of an underground resistance," he said. "We keep alive the one fundamental thing that makes us human and protect it at all costs. The thing naïve people try to erase because they don't understand it nor our methods."

He watched my face.

"The human mind."

The words felt obscene in his mouth.

"The human mind? You mean people?," I said.

"In this world," he said, "not long after infancy, the brain is removed from the body and placed into a manufactured shell."

My stomach lurched. "That's madness."

"It's the only way humans can survive. It's freedom."

"The people outside," I said slowly, "they aren't…"

"Mostly shells," he said. "Human minds inside machine bodies."

I thought of the knights breaking apart. Sparks where blood should have been.

He glanced at the suit I wore.

"That's why the body still resembles the shape of man. Illusion matters. If we alter the shape too far from man, the brain goes into shock."

The room went silent.

Above us, the city screamed again.

Elit exhaled.

Decision made.

"Come," he said.

He pressed his palm to a seam in the wall.

And the room opened.

Behind it waited a narrow opening and a spiral stair that dropped into darkness like a throat.

We descended.

Each step took us farther from the noise above, but also farther from the light. The air grew cooler and damp. The walls changed, less polished, more honest. Stone and old metal.

After a long stretch, the stair released us into a chamber lit by dim, steady lamps. Not candles, but close enough that my body almost believed it.

People turned toward us.

Faces. Real faces.

Shock first.

Then hunger, but not for food.

Hope.

"One of us," someone whispered, as if saying it too loud would break it. "Another Human of Flesh."

A man stepped forward, eyes wide, too bright with excitement. "Hi," he blurted. "I am Quincy. What is your name?"

He extended his hand.

My voice came out thin. "Gregory."

The old man lifted a hand. Gentle. Firm.

"Easy," he said. "He needs to breathe before you bury him with questions."

"I just wanted to check his grip," Quincy speaking like he was reporting.

He guided me down a short hallway lined with small rooms. Tight. Plain. Functional. A bunker carved into the earth.

At the end he opened a door.

A small bed. Clean sheets. A narrow glass stall in the corner that looked like a window turned inward.

"Rest," he said. "We will speak again when you have slept."

My mouth opened. A dozen questions fought to be first.

But exhaustion hit all at once, heavy and sudden, like the future itself had weight.

"And that," he added, nodding toward the glass stall, "is a shower."

I stared. "How does it work?"

"Step inside," he said. "Press the button."

"No soap?"

He almost smiled. Almost.

"You will see."

He closed the door behind him.

I undressed and folded the dark suit like it might bite me if I treated it too casually. I stepped into the glass stall. The door shut with a soft seal. I held my breath and pressed the button.

Steam swallowed me.

Panic surged. For half a second I thought it was another trap, another net.

Then I smelled it.

Like a world of peace and lavender.

Warmth settled over my skin, gentle as breath.

And then the steam vanished, pulled away so fast it felt like it had been stolen back into the ceiling.

I looked down.

The dirt was gone.

The stink of war was gone.

My skin was clean. Dry. Smooth.

I put my hands to my face and the glass splinters were gone.

Weeks of marching and blood and smoke had been erased in a heartbeat.

The subtle green glow was now clear as glass. A dust of emeralds sparkled in my pores. They were no doubt a part of me now. Like a tattoo.

"What kind of…" I whispered. The word magic would not come.

There was a new set of clothes folded on a dresser. The white garments looked a little like a gown, but they were clean and exactly my size.

I dressed again and sat on the bed.

The sheets were soft. The air smelled clean. The room was underground and cramped, but compared to the city above, it felt like sanctuary.

I lay back and stared at the ceiling.

For the first time since the battlefield, my eyes closed and my body loosened.

And for one fragile moment, I felt something close to peace.

Little did I know, it would be the last time I ever slept.

Chapter Five
LIKE NEW

"Gregory. Open your eyes."

The voice pulled me up like a hook.

Confusion hit first, then light. I blinked against a harsh glare, a white disk hanging above me like a small, cruel sun. I was not in the room where I had fallen asleep.

I tried to sit up.

My body did not answer.

I tried again, harder, and only my eyes moved. Left. Right. That was all.

Panic surged, the old animal part of me clawing at the walls, but it had nowhere to go. My chest did not heave. My pulse did not race. The fear hit and slid off, like water on glass. My stomach did not drop.

Two figures stood over me in white gowns. Their faces were hidden behind clear masks that reflected the overhead light in hard, bright shapes. They did not shift their weight. They did not blink. They looked less like people and more like instruments arranged above a table.

"Gregory," one of them said. Calm. Flat. "I'm Doctor Quincy."

His name landed and I recognized it. The man who had shaken my hand underground. The man who looked harmless.

This Quincy was horror.

"You cannot move right now," he continued. "The interface is stabilizing. Do not attempt voluntary motion."

Inter…face…?

The word cut deeper than any blade. My thoughts skittered, searching for a world where that word belonged, and finding none.

My mind slammed against my skull, furious, trying to drag my body into revolt.

Nothing followed.

"What did you do to me," I tried to say.

No sound came out. My throat did not form it. My lips did not shape it. The question stayed trapped in my head like a scream behind glass.

Quincy leaned closer, studying my eyes as if they were gauges.

"We finished the procedure," he said.

Procedure?

Cold water. A bucket poured down my spine.

A sheet covered me from the neck down. I tried to look, but my neck would not bend. I could not even twitch a shoulder. I could only stare upward into the light and feel the sting of being awake inside something that refused to be mine.

Something was different in my sight.

Edges were sharper than they should have been. Colors looked separated from each other, not blended. When my gaze moved, it moved smoothly, without the small jumps of fatigue or the quiver of fear. Even my own focus felt engineered.

A spark of terror tried to ignite.

It blinked out.

My mind rejected it, not as denial, but as if the fuel for fear was missing.

Quincy's voice returned, measured, almost bored with its own miracle.

"We successfully removed your brain and placed it into your new home."

The words should have split me open.

They should have made me thrash. Curse. Beg. The old Gregory would have broken Quincy's teeth with my fist.

Instead, the sentence dropped into me like a stone into deep water.

I understood it.

I waited for the wave.

Nothing came.

My outrage was there, somewhere, but it felt distant. Delayed. Like it belonged to a man I used to be, and I was only remembering how he would have reacted.

Quincy watched me carefully.

Not with pity.

With interest.

"We ran diagnostics," he said. "Cognition is intact. Memory appears stable. Your neural patterns are merging cleanly with the chassis."

Chassis.

He said it the way a carpenter says wood.

The other masked figure spoke, softer but no warmer.

"We are relocating you to recovery."

Two more figures entered. They moved with routine purpose, hands quiet, steps practiced. They did not look at my face as if there was a person behind it. They looked at me the way men look at cargo.

The bed began to move.

The doors ahead opened without a touch, folding apart like soldiers welcoming a king.

We passed into a corridor so bright it hurt to look at, all white surfaces, glossy and clean. The ceiling glowed from within, and a thin line of light zigzagged down the length of the hall like a vein. An esthetic fixture in such a sterile and cold place.

They put me into a room that was also white, but arranged to imitate comfort. A soft chair. A smooth table. A wall panel that looked almost like a window if you did not look too hard.

A meager attempt of warmth.

The suggestion of a home.

They stopped my bed and stepped back.

"Someone will check on you," one said, knowing I was going to be there for a long time.

They left.

The door shut on its own with a quiet final sound.

I was alone.

My thoughts moved differently now. Fast, organized. I could not move anything but my eyes, but my senses had sharpened into something unnatural.

I listened.

I could hear tiny impacts far down the hall. The soft hiss of air through vents. The electrical commotion behind the walls. The building's breathing. Even the silence had texture, layered with sound I never would have noticed before.

And then I realized what was missing.

My lungs did not beg for breath.

My eyes did not demand blinking.

My heart did not announce itself.

My skin did not itch. My stomach did not ache. No hunger. No thirst. No fatigue. No pain.

The body that used to argue with every moment of existence had gone quiet.

My emotions still existed, but they had nowhere to land. Fear arrived and found no racing pulse to ride. Anger flared and found no heat in my blood. Grief came and found no throat to tighten around it.

My thoughts were just pictures now.

Clear, sharp pictures.

With no weight behind them. No physical flitch or wince. A one-way conversation.

I thought, I want to go home.

The thought should have broken me.

It did not.

It simply sat there, clean and flat, like text on a page.

My body had become a room with the lantern out.

And I was trapped inside it, watching.

Chapter Six
TRAINING BEGINS

The double doors swung open.

Two people stepped in side by side, moving in perfect sync. They marched to my bedside and stopped as if they had been placed there, one on my right, one on my left.

"Hello, Gregory," the one to my right said. "Your training begins."

Before I could even process, my bed lifted.

A gentle jolt ran through the frame, and the whole thing rose a few inches higher. I had not realized that this bed has been floating, levitating. It pivoted toward the doorway on its own.

The two men kept pace at my sides, hands clasped behind their backs, never touching the bed.

And the bed followed.

We entered the hallway at a quick, steady pace. I flicked my gaze left and right, trying to steal glimpses through the narrow windows set into the doors as we passed.

But we were moving too fast and there were too many doors.

Panic tried to rise, but it came sluggishly, like a reflex caught in quicksand.

The corridor felt endless. Door after door. Room after room. The number of them was unbelievable.

Then we passed a doorway marked PHASE I, and two more men emerged, guiding another floating stretcher and a following cart.

For half a second, I had a clear view.

A sheet covered a patient. The outline beneath it was unmistakably a human body…

…with no head.

I looked away quickly on instinct. But then curiosity made me look back.

On a separate cart sat a glass jar.

Inside it floated a brain.

Thin cords, like veins, ran from the jar into a box below. The liquid around the brain glowed faintly, thick and slow, and pulses of blue light shivered through it in steady rhythm, like breathing.

Disgusting.

The stretcher and cart vanished behind us. My bed kept floating. The men kept marching.

At last we reached another set of double doors.

They swung open as we arrived.

What waited on the other side did not feel like a room.

It felt like a world.

The ceiling rose into a smooth white dome, stretching so far it looked like a horizon. The light was clean and endless.

The doors shut behind us.

Then the men at my sides stepped away.

"Rise," a voice commanded.

It did not come from a mouth. It came from everywhere. From the dome itself.

And without effort, without even needing to think about it, I sat up and threw the sheet aside.

I swung my legs over the edge of the floating bed and stepped onto the floor.

My mind stalled.

I looked down, bracing myself for metal, seams, some monstrous shape.

But I looked the same.

Arms. Hands. Skin.

My body.

Exactly as I remembered it.

Then I saw the golden glow.

A soft golden city of lights lived beneath my skin, like fireflies in a jar. When I moved, it rippled across me in gentle waves, like fluttering butterflies, rising and falling with each motion.

I turned my hands slowly, watching the flow of lights swim over my knuckles and along my wrists, like schools of glittering fish.

I could not look away.

I tested my joints.

My shoulders rolled without resistance. My spine twisted smoothly, like wringing a towel. I turned my head to the right, expecting the familiar stop, the tug of muscle, the warning edge of pain.

It did not stop.

It kept turning.

Smooth as a wheel.

Past the limit.

Past the place where bone should catch and protest.

The world spun around me, and in one impossible motion I came full circle until I was staring straight ahead again.

A full turn.

As if my head were the needle of a compass, and someone spun my body.

I lifted my hands and rotated my wrists. A full circle, easy as turning a key.

I clenched my fingers into a fist, then opened them again.

They bent farther than they should have.

Too far.

I folded my hand back until my fingertips brushed my forearm.

No strain.

Only obedient motion.

I looked up.

I was alone.

Snow-blinded by white.

Then the voice returned, calm and certain, as if the dome itself were speaking down into my skull.

"Gregory. Welcome to your body."

A pause, like the world taking a breath.

"You were selected."

The words settled heavy, and still I could not decide whether they felt like honor or a sentence.

"You were selected to stand among the elite," the voice continued. "Warriors tasked with saving humankind and the Earth. You possess battlefield intelligence. A mind fit to lead."

"You are mistaken," I said. "I am no great warrior."

The confession tasted bitter. It was the only truth I still had.

"In my last battle I was cold. Tired. We were ambushed." I swallowed hard. "My heart wasn't in the fight. I let my brothers down."

"Though you were tired, broken, and worn, you never quit," the voice answered. "You fought back."

My thoughts snagged.

How does it know?

"You fought even when fear gripped you," it said. "You fought even when you no longer cared whether you lived or…"

I cut in, almost pleading. "Exactly. I was finished, I surrendered. Not on the battlefield, but to myself. I did not care if I lived or died."

"That," the voice said, "is the mind of a true warrior."

I stared at my hands as the gold light moved under my skin, and something in me twisted.

"A coward hides until the noise passes," the voice went on. "But you chose to rise…to return fire."

Then, colder, like judgment:

"And you were Human of Flesh. You felt hunger. Cold. Pain. Exhaustion."

I swallowed.

"With those burdens removed," the voice said, "you will be unstoppable. It is your mind that makes you a warrior. Not your body. Not your ailments. Not what your flesh demands. Your mind."

My throat tightened around the words I had been holding back since the first day I opened my eyes in the future.

"But my wife," I whispered. "My children."

The sentence came out smaller than I meant it to.

"I left them behind. I died on that battlefield." My voice cracked. "I will never see them again."

The dome above me shifted.

The white drained away. Darkness spilled across the ceiling until the room felt like night.

Then an image appeared overhead.

My wife.

My children.

My knees hit the floor before I chose to fall.

Seeing them, truly seeing them, tore something open in me. My body gave me nothing. No tears. No shaking breath. No heaving chest.

But my mind raced until it hurt.

A wound in a place I did not know could bleed.

The images changed.

My children sat inside our wooden shack by candlelight. The light was low, but it gilded their faces. My son, seven years old, held the book I used to read to him at night.

He couldn't read, or even speak, but he loved to flip through the pages. My daughter, 5 years old, sat beside him, smiling and watching him with love and admiration. She truly cared for him, you can see it in the way her eyes sparkled in the candlelight.

A dread crawled through my thoughts.

He flapped his arms with excitement and his elbow struck the candle.

The flame caught what lay on the table.

It climbed fast and sudden.

My daughter screamed.

My son froze, eyes wide, too young to understand how quickly fire becomes death.

The blaze swallowed the room.

The image went dark.

Then I saw my wife outside in the night, snow falling gently around her. She stood on the porch with a quilt pulled tight. The windows behind her glowed dimly.

She heard the scream.

She turned.

She threw the door open and ran inside.

Smoke poured out.

Flames rolled through the house as if the walls were made of oil and paper.

She vanished into dark smoke coughing and screaming, a blood curdling scream, the worst kind of scream. From a mother in grief, "Thomas! Sarah!"

The ceiling went black again.

A sound tore out of me, half growl, half prayer.

I slammed my fist into the floor.

The surface cracked beneath my knuckles.

Memories surged. Me reading to my son at night. My voice calming him. That same book in his hands.

And now I could do nothing.

I was trapped in a shell in an alien age, separated by impossible distance and time. No word I spoke could bridge it. No thought could reach them.

Everything I had was gone.

Country. Family. Choice.

All I had left were my thoughts.

I stayed on my knees in the ruin of myself, waiting for grief to finish what the bullet started.

It didn't.

The voice returned, steady as iron.

"It is time to begin."

I stood, not to obey, but because there was nothing left to hold on to. Hollow. Scraped clean.

And in that emptiness, one thing remained.

If I can't return, and they're truly gone, then I'll carry them in my heart. I'll stop grieving with words. I'll do it with war.

The vow settled in me like a nail driven home.

Heat gathered behind my eyes. My hands clenched without trembling. Somewhere inside this borrowed body, something answered.

My glow brightened.

The white dome shimmered.

The vast room dissolved, and a new world formed around me.

Trees and brush rose from nothing, thick and green like the forests I remembered.

A musket appeared, leaning against a tree.

"Pick up your weapon," the voice commanded.

I stepped forward and took it.

The wood was familiar beneath my hands. The weight. The balance. I'd carried a musket for miles until it stopped feeling like a weapon and started feeling like an extension of my arm.

In the Continental Army, no one reloaded faster than I did.

The moment the stock settled into my shoulder, something in me went quiet. It was like stepping into a room only I could enter.

Maybe that's why they dug me up.

Not because I was special.

Because I was useful. A killer. A warrior.

A rustle sounded in the distance.

I turned.

Chapter Seven
Armored

The doors I had entered through reappeared at once. They opened on their own, and the same two guards stepped out, moving in perfect step. With a simple gesture, they signaled for me to follow.

I walked through the door and down the corridor with one on my left and one on my right. We had no need to hurry. Time felt endless here, stretched thin and quiet.

At last we reached a door that looked fortified, heavier than the others, with dark seams and metal locks that suggested it was meant to keep something in, or keep something out. It opened, and we entered.

Inside was a glass chamber.

It reminded me of the shower I had been given when I first met those so-called "resistance" people. But this box was larger, and at its center sat a chair.

One of the guards pointed. "Sit."

I obeyed. I stepped into the chamber, took a seat, and the glass door sealed shut behind me.

From outside, one of them pressed a button.

Fog poured in, thick and swirling. It wrapped around my body and clung to my skin. At first it felt like cool mist, then like something finer, almost alive, threading over me in invisible strands. The fog shifted colors as it moved, turning and deepening like stained light through water.

Then it tightened.

Not painfully. But with intention. Like vines taking hold.

I tried to move, but the sensation held me in place, weaving and shaping itself around my limbs, my chest, my shoulders.

And then the fog cleared as suddenly as it had come.

I looked down.

I was encased in armor.

It was the same kind the guards had worn when they dragged me into that floating iron "cannonball," except the light that traced through it was not the ember-orange I remembered. This glow was emerald green, pulsing faintly beneath the surface.

I stood up.

The armor was weightless. I moved as if it were not separate from me at all, as if it had become a second skin. When I lifted my arms, it lifted with me without a sound, without resistance, perfectly obedient.

One of the guards watched, then spoke.

"This is your armor," he said. "Treat it with respect, and it will respect you."

He paused, and his voice lowered, almost like warning.

"This armor protects only what is worth protecting."

He crossed to the corner of the room and opened a glass cabinet. Inside were rows of glowing cups filled with a thick gel that shimmered with trapped lightning. I recognized them at once. They were the same strange drinks I had seen in the city when I was running for my life.

He took one cup and carried it to me with steady hands.

"Drink."

I stared at it. It did not look like water. It did not look like any juice or ale I had ever known. The gel inside swirled slowly, lit from within.

I should have refused.

But I was too deep in this. And something in me had learned to just go with the flow.

I took the cup and raised it to my lips.

The moment the gel touched my mouth, I did not truly swallow. It slid into me as if my body pulled it down on its own. A cold spark raced through my veins.

My suit of armor lit up.

Emerald light surged across the armor in branching lines, bright for an instant, then gone as quickly as it had come.

And a new sensation spread through me.

My senses sharpened until the air felt loud. My movements became lighter, quicker. My body responded before I could even think. For the first time since waking in this future, I felt connected to myself, as if mind, body, and armor had finally locked together.

The guards nodded, satisfied.

"Follow," one said.

The doors opened. We stepped out again, one guard on my left, one on my right, guiding me down the long corridor.

We passed a crossing hallway, and as I glanced down it, I caught a glimpse of someone.

A familiar shape. A familiar beard.

My chest tightened.

The old man.

Before I could stop myself, anger flared. I twisted away from the guards and sprinted down the side hall.

"Gregory!" one of them barked behind me.

They chased, but my new body moved like wind. The gel burned clean through me, turning thought into motion. I ran past door after door, each with a small window set in the metal.

I looked.

Empty rooms. Bright rooms. Beds and glass and white walls.

Then, through one small pane, I saw him.

The old man stood inside, facing the door, as if he had been waiting. He smiled.

Something in me snapped.

I pounded on the door. Once. Twice. Again, harder, until my fist ached from the impact.

The lock released and the door slid open.

I stormed in and closed the distance in two strides, raising my hand to strike him.

"Stop," the voice from above commanded.

My body froze mid-motion.

Blue lightning wrapped around me, pinning my limbs the way the iron dog had. I could not move, but I could still speak, and the words poured out of me like fire.

"You betrayed me," I shouted. "You called yourself resistance. I trusted you! You turned me into a monster! You traitor!"

The old man's smile did not fade.

Instead, his shape wavered.

His skin shimmered.

Not like sweat. Like a surface deciding what it wanted to be.

For half a second his face didn't fit. It slid, imperfectly aligned, and something underneath pressed forward as if there was another face behind his skin.

Red scales rose in a pattern protruding out of his flesh, and his human skin vanished like draining water through cloth.

I met his eyes. The pupils narrowed into thin black cuts. A second lid swept across, clear and quick, like a blink of a snake.

Then the face, like molding clay, shifted and formed to sealed itself again.

He returned to the old man again, calm as ever, as if shaking off a sneeze.

"I am part of the resistance," he said. "Not against the Order. Not against humankind."

I stared, helpless, rage boiling in my thoughts.

"I resist my own kind."

"What are you," I rasped.

He stepped closer, and his voice softened.

"I am a Reptilian. A race of interstellar beings who know only violence," he said. "They want conquest. They want control. They kill with little reason."

His eyes held mine through the crackling blue light.

"But I…"

He paused and locked his gaze on me.

"I do not want death. My heart does not tempt me to *take*. It beats to *give*. I want to protect. That is what *resistance* means to me. I resist my natural expectation. I resist the Reptilians."

He lifted a hand, slow, as if calming an animal.

"I did not lure you with lies," he said. "There was no hidden veil. You were taken because you are rare. Your will was proven in flesh."

He paused.

"Your mind deserved to be unburdened by flesh."

My eyes widened and I exhaled as if receiving a blow to the gut.

"Now is your time to be reborn," he said. "Leave your past behind and let it guide you into the future."

"Your family, for example," he continued, "was innocent. They did not die by accident."

The words hit me harder than the lightning.

"They were destroyed," he said, "because a government tore you from your home and forced you into a war that was never truly yours."

"Do you not do the same?" I demanded. "How is this different?"

The old man began to answer, but I cut him off.

"No. Do not tell me it is not the same," I said. "You say you took my body and placed me into another so I might 'defend' humans. But that is exactly what happened in my own time."

My voice rose, sharp with a fury I could finally recognize.

"In my land, we fought to defend what was ours. Independence. Freedom. We marched not because we were dragged in chains, but because our own will chose it."

I leaned forward as far as the blue lightning would allow.

"What you have done to me is *not* my will," I said. "You may call it defense, but at *my* expense."

The old man's expression did not change, but his eyes sharpened.

"You believe it was *your* will to fight," he said. "You believe it was *your* will to leave your family. *Your* will to march. *Your* will to die."

He stepped closer, voice low and steady.

"Tell me, Gregory. Where did that *will* come from? Who stirred it in you? Who spoke the words that made you and your neighbors burn with purpose?"

He let the questions hang, one after another, like blows.

"What smooth tongue roused your friends? Your family? What voice gathered you all together and pointed you toward a common enemy?"

His gaze held mine.

"Was it truly your own idea," he asked, "or did someone place that idea in your head and teach you to call it yours?"

"Was your life ever truly in danger?" he asked. "Was your family truly at risk?"

His voice stayed calm, but each question cut deeper.

"What was the cause? What was it for?"

He tilted his head slightly, studying me.

"And if your friends had not joined the fight, would you have gone alone? Would you have stayed home?"

He let out a slow breath.

"Or did everyone simply follow the next man, one after another, until marching felt like the only choice left?"

to drop you without tearing you apart. Meant to make you disappear."

My mouth went numb.

"You shot me," I whispered.

He did not deny it.

"I put you down," he said. "I chose the only outcome where you did not die for real."

My throat went dry as ash. My thoughts tripped over each other, searching for something to hold onto, but every answer led to the same place.

The same face. The same calm.

The same man who had pulled me out of my own fire and then lit another one under me again.

I swallowed hard, forcing the next question past my teeth.

"If you can shape yourself into any figure," I said, "why do you wear the face of an old man?"

His gaze dropped.

"I wear this shape," he said, "because it is the face of the last Human of Flesh I put down."

The words struck me.

He lifted his chin, and for the first time his voice carried something like shame.

"I keep it in his honor. And as punishment. What I did was wrong. He was honorable. Intelligent. Moral. A man who shaped minds and created freedom of thought for anyone who would listen. He was not a warrior, but a scholar."

My hands curled into fists.

"You speak of him like he mattered to you."

"He did," the old man said. "More than you know."

Then he looked straight at me.

"He was your son."

The room seemed to tilt.

"My son?"

"That's impossible," I said as the world narrowed. "They told me that he died in a fire…"

I shook my head, dizzy with rage and disbelief. "…And…a scholar?" I said. "That's impossible! Lies! He couldn't speak…Mute! He was always twitching and never looked anyone in the eye. Something was wrong with him!"

My voice sharpened. "What potential did you see in him?"

"He could not speak," the old man said, "because he spent years listening."

His voice grew quieter, almost reverent.

"Observing. Learning. Developing a mind in silence while others wasted theirs in noise. He became something rare, even among Humans of Flesh."

Something inside me cracked.

For the first time in this cold, engineered body, a wave of sorrow hit so hard it felt like being split open. Not numbness. Not distant thought.

Real grief.

The old man's expression tightened.

"And…He did not die in the fire," the old man said. "I saved him."

The words hit me like a blow.

"What?" I rasped. "You mean you *saved* my son?"

"Yes." His voice didn't change. "I pulled him from the fire."

My throat locked. "And my wife? My daughter?"

He held my gaze a fraction too long. When his eyes dropped, it wasn't shame. It was genuine pain and grief.

"I couldn't," he said quietly. "Not without being seen."

I trembled. "Why?"

He drew a slow breath, like he had rehearsed this confession and still hated it.

"Because the fire spread too fast," he said. "Because your daughter was too small. The smoke already overcome her. And because I was not free."

I tried to take a step toward him before I could think, but the blue lightning still gripped me. "Not free?"

He looked back up, and there was regret there, heavy and worn down by years.

"At that time, I was still a Reptilian Enforcer," he said. "A soldier. I was monitored and watched. Even then. Putting my location at risk to save your son was a chance. If I stayed longer, if I made it obvious, I would have been exposed, and your son would have been executed."

The room felt tighter. Like the air itself was listening.

"I vanished," he continued. "I went off-grid. That moment set this whole operation in motion."

A pause. Then, smaller:

"I'm sorry."

The apology hit worse than the answer.

I swallowed and forced my voice to work, but nothing came out.

Elit continued.

"Your village was my post."

He stepped closer.

"I was sent to observe humanity and report back," he said. "Back then, we couldn't seize an entire population and harvest it. Not yet. We were still developing. Still studying the logistics. The travel. The transport. Even among ourselves, we fought over Earth the moment we arrived. Different factions. Different claims."

His voice tightened, and something hard settled behind his eyes.

"So we did what we could do. We proceeded with our assignments and blended in."

He lifted a hand, almost dismissive of the skin he wore.

"We shapeshift. We wear human faces to move among you. Merchants. Leaders. Soldiers. Preachers. Businessmen."

He looked away, like the words tasted like rust.

"We used your own hands to build the world we meant to inherit. We steered development. We kept the obedient alive and the brilliant quiet. And when unrest showed its first spark, we crushed it before it could catch."

I felt sick, even if my body refused to show it.

"A lot of great minds were sacrificed," he said. "Not because they were dangerous with weapons, but because they were dangerous with ideas. People who could have changed a century…silenced before they spoke too loudly. Erased before they could be remembered."

His eyes returned to mine.

"There is blood on our hands," he said. "More than I can count."

He swallowed, and his lip trembled. Then his eyes focused with determination.

"That's what changed me."

"Our operation on Earth was delicate," he continued. "Emerald One could not be allowed to fall into human hands. If your kind discovered it first, you would use it against us. So it became a race. We advanced our technology while making sure you did not."

He leaned in, as if the stone walls might carry his confession.

"You are stubborn creatures," he said. "When threatened, you band together. Your will is fierce. However, it is also a weakness. When threatened, humans never form just one group, but two or three. The original threat gets lost and forgotten, and a new one eats you from the inside."

His gaze held mine.

There was a long stretch of silence. And in the silence, my mind couldn't shake the fact that I was looking at the shape of my aged son. The embers of guilt and regret grew into a flame.

The blue lightning around me vanished. My body was released. My knees gave out and I fell to the floor.

The flame grew.

Why…why did I not see what Elit saw in my son? I just saw a burden…a mute. Elit saw a scholar…a visionary.

I wanted my son, Thomas, to speak. I wanted my boy to lift his head and answer me, to prove he was there, to prove he was whole. Frustration filled me so sharply it felt like teeth in my mind. In our village, no one understood his silence. They called it a curse. They called my wife and me sinners.

They looked at him with pity, or fear, or both.

And I did too.

I thought it was a flaw. A weakness. The devil. A punishment.

Only now did I understand that I was mistaken.

What I had feared and hated in him was his greatest strength.

The thought struck me with a shame that burned even through numb flesh.

I had failed him.

I had failed as a father.

I looked up at the old man.

And I saw what I had not seen before.

Burn marks.

Scars, half-hidden beneath wrinkles and shadow, etched into the skin like old fire. My eyes traced the lines across his face, and suddenly I could not unsee it. Beneath the age, beneath the disguise, there were shapes that echoed my own. A familiar curve. A familiar brow. Like looking at a reflection that had been broken and remade.

"You have forsaken me," Elit said in the voice of a little 7-year-old boy.

My suit flared beneath the surface, light surging in uneven waves.

The two guards jerked backward, startled.

The old man watched me, intrigued, as if he had been waiting for this.

A storm rose in my mind.

Anger surged through me. The armor answered it, the emerald glow fading as a red heat crept across my chest and down my arms.

Rage blossomed in me like never before.

Rage at myself. Rage at Elit. Rage for rage's sake.

I looked the old man dead in the eyes and charged.

I drew my fist back and swung for his head.

My blow met nothing.

He slipped beneath it like smoke, and my fist drove past where his skull had been, smashing into the wall hard enough to leave a crater.

He reappeared at once, not as himself, but as my wife.

For a heartbeat, my mind recoiled.

Then fury snapped it clean in half.

I knew that face was not hers. It was a mockery. A mask meant to soften me, to unmake me.

I rushed the image and struck again.

My shoulder passed through her like fog, and I slammed into the wall behind, carving another crater into the white surface.

He appeared again, this time in his true form. The reptilian creature, lean and horned, its skin scaled and red, eyes black with something older than men.

I attacked him again and again.

Each time he slid under my blows like a snake across the floor, always just beyond my reach. He never struck back. He only evaded, parried, moved. As if he wanted me to spend myself empty.

It was useless.

I was strong, but I was powerless.

And as the rage burned, something colder seeped in beneath it. Hopelessness. The realization of how trapped I truly was.

Trapped in a body that was not mine. In a world I did not belong to. Among people I could not trust.

Even death felt far away, as if it had been locked out of me.

My thoughts turned bleak and morbid, but my body remained hollow. I carried a storm of anger with nowhere for it to go.

My knees hit the floor.

I bowed my head and began to pray. The words left my mouth like dust, barely more than a whisper.

The creature turned its back on me.

It stood there still, hands at its sides, as if it had already won.

I looked up.

Something in me moved without permission. Not thought. Not choice. A final, violent impulse.

I surged to my feet and drove my fist forward.

It punched through his back and burst out the other side.

He gasped.

For the first time, his body carried weight. The weight of real flesh. The weight of dying.

I stared at my arm buried in him, stunned by what I had done and by how easily it had happened. Then I ripped my hand free.

The reptile staggered, sank to his knees, and toppled onto his side.

With what little strength remained, he turned his head toward me.

His eyes met mine.

"I'm sorry," he said.

Then his eyes closed.

Regret hit me harder than rage. The red light bleeding through my suit faded and vanished as if it had never been there.

I stared at the creature on the floor, my arm still trembling from what I'd done. This was the one who saved my son. The one who pulled him from the fire. The one who saw something in him worth preserving.

And I had driven my fist through his back like an animal.

My mind felt clouded, my judgment ruined. I didn't know who to trust. Everything around me felt unreal, like living inside a nightmare that refused to end. I was trapped in a cage with no door and no exit, rage and grief circling inside me with nowhere to go.

I lunged to his side and dropped to my knees. I pressed my hands to the wound.

Sorrow surged through me so hard it almost made sound. The armor answered it.

Red light flared beneath my skin, brighter than before. It flooded across my arms and spilled into the air in thin branching lines. Red lightning leapt from my hands and wrapped around the reptile's body, buzzing and snapping like a living thing.

The light grew, swelling until it became a fog that consumed us both.

Then, as suddenly as it came, it vanished.

The creature convulsed once.

The torn flesh drew together. The wound sealed shut as if stitched by invisible hands. He went still.

Then his eyes opened, slow and steady.

He looked at me.

And with a voice like quiet triumph, he said, "I knew you could do it."

The world tilted. My knees buckled. I collapsed.

Chapter Eight

TEAM

My eyes opened slowly, and my body felt heavy. For the first time, I could feel the true weight of the machine I was trapped inside. My mind ordered my limbs to move, and after a moment of stubborn stillness, they obeyed.

I sat up and swung my legs over the edge of the bed.

Vine-like ropes, woven like horsehair, penetrated my wrists. I yanked them free, first the left, then the right. They snapped back with a slick, living recoil, retreating into a box beside me like a snake sliding into its hole. An energetic light inside the box flickered, dulled, and finally died down, accompanied by a soft suctioning whisper.

This room was different.

Dim. Quiet. Calm in a way I haven't seen in this world, yet.

It looked to be night.

The room was small. A few glass cabinets stood along one side, their surfaces glossy and dark, reflecting light without revealing what lay within.

Ahead of me was a large circular window. The source of the room's light.

I walked toward it, each step answered by the tired clank of metal. The suit felt less like armor now and more like an iron maiden shut around my soul.

A low rumble filled the room as I reached the glass, gentle enough to soothe rather than threaten.

And then I saw it.

Thousands upon thousands of stars spilled across the dark, bright as scattered salt. There was no ground. No water. No trees. Only endless distance.

Rocks and scraps of metal drifted past the window, slow and silent, like debris carried along by an invisible river.

Far off, clouds of color pulsed in the distance, breathing and turning, stretching like living ribbons. It was unearthly.

And yet, for the first time in what felt like forever, peace settled over me.

The door behind me slid open.

I snapped my head.

Elit entered.

"Good morning, Gregory," he said. He crossed the room and sat in the corner with a careful ease.

I kept my gaze on the stars. "What is this place?"

"We are in deep space," he replied. "Headed to your first mission."

My eyes narrowed. "What mission?"

"You will learn soon." His voice remained calm. "We arrive in about a week. You have already been unconscious for two."

"Two weeks," I repeated, tasting the words.

"You exhausted yourself reviving me," Elit said.

"I didn't mean to," I said. "I didn't even know I could. It just… happened."

Elit was quiet for a moment. Then he spoke again, lower, almost thoughtful.

"There have always been whispers," he said. "Old rumors. The kind men laugh at in daylight and ponder alone at night. That Emerald One can pull a soul back from the edge."

He watched me as he spoke, like he was taking inventory.

"I never had certainty," he went on. "Only a theory sharp enough to cut, and a faith ugly enough to use. So I buried you."

The words sat between us, calm and poisonous.

"In all my years, I saw Emerald One used the way everyone uses it. Physically. Chemically. Ground down and compressed, then coaxed awake with a spark so its power spills out on command. Forced through a circuit. They call it Emerald Ignition." His mouth barely moved when he smiled.

He tilted his head, listening to something in me.

"You waking in the soil was my first proof," he said. "A success."

Silence.

"Then, now, you revived *me*," he said, and the word revived sounded measured, tested. "Even with no stone physically in your hand."

His gaze fixed, hungry now.

"Counting me, that makes two successful Emerald One revivals."

He stepped closer. His voice softened, not kinder, but sharper. More exact.

"The common denominator is you." Elit looked at the green glow pulsing through the seams of my armor.

"Emerald One is prized for energy," he said. "For lights. For machines. For war. But you found something hidden, undiscovered, underneath all that."

He tapped his chest once, like knocking on a sealed door.

"You didn't just reach for the stone," he said. "You aligned your will, your emotion, and Emerald One's sacred charge, and something buried inside it answered."

He smiled, thin.

"That's the kind of thing people swear happens in legends."

His gaze went hungry.

"Now it's standing in front of me."

He held my gaze.

"Together we will achieve many great things."

"Tell me, Gregory." He said slowly. "What do you feel... when you let it in?"

"Nothing," I said. My voice sounded thin in the room. "Nothing I can name."

I swallowed.

"It only happens when I'm... not myself. When something in me breaks loose." I stared at my hands. "Before I woke underground, I saw my family. Clear as daylight." My throat tightened. "And when I put my hand on you, I was furious and burned by dark guilt."

Elit's eyes did not leave me.

"Good," he said softly.

He stepped closer, and when he spoke again his words were careful, built for a man from 1776.

"Inside your body is a center," he said. "A distribution point. A heart, in the way your new body understands the word."

He held two fingers close together, showing a size no bigger than a musket ball.

"It carries a condensed seed of Emerald One," he said. "Small. Dense. Enough to power everything you are now, and keep your mind tethered to this shell."

He paused, watching my face for comprehension, for fear, for anything he could measure.

"When you draw on it lightly, it lasts," he continued. "You can walk. You can fight. You can exist."

His voice lowered.

"But when you reach the way you did, when you revived me, you do not sip from it. You empty it."

He watched to make sure I followed.

"And when it empties," Elit said, "it must be charged again."

As he spoke, something beyond the window caught my eye.

A bright strand of light cut across the stars, swift and silent, like a burning thread pulled through dark cloth. It vanished as quickly as it came, and for a heartbeat the room felt smaller, as if the sky itself had leaned closer to listen.

Elit also saw the strand of light, "Those are my friends."

He paused.

"Anyway…Emerald One decays," Elit continued. "It runs out. And when it does, your body fails, unless it is replaced."

They brought me back. So, if I were worthless to them, I would already be gone. If they need to charge me once in a while, or change my battery…let 'em.

They needed me.

Elit's gaze stayed on my face, like he was watching for cracks.

"You put a great strain on your supply," he said. "We have been keeping you stable."

He lifted a hand and pointed at my wrists.

"That's how we recharge your system."

My eyes flicked back to the window.

"Now what?" I asked.

Elit's mouth moved into something that almost resembled a smile.

"I want you to meet your team," he said.

He turned toward the door.

"Follow me."

The door slid open, and Elit stepped out first. I followed. We turned left into a corridor shaped like the inside of a barrel, its walls curving smoothly overhead until they met again. Oval windows ran along the right side in a neat line, each one framed in dark metal.

Beyond the glass was only the deep, black void, littered with drifting rock and silent scraps of metal. Every so often a distant cluster of stars slipped past, bright and cold. The sight should have stirred wonder in me. It did not. It was simply there, moving as the ship moved.

Our footsteps rang against the floor in hollow taps and tired clanks. Elit's steps were light. Mine sounded heavier, the suit answering each motion like a restrained animal.

At the end of the hall, the corridor widened into a larger chamber.

A round table sat at the center, polished so dark it nearly swallowed the light. Chairs circled it, each mounted to a hidden track. They rotated slowly, as if to greet me.

Above the table, the ceiling rose high into a dome, and directly overhead a wide circular window opened onto the stars. The glow from it fell straight down onto the table like a pale spotlight.

Elit stopped beside one of the chairs and looked toward the places around it.

At the far end of the table sat two men.

They were the same two who had guarded me in the facility.

Only now their masks were gone.

They sat plainly, shoulders squared, faces uncovered, as if the sight of them should have comforted me. It did not. Without the helmets they looked almost ordinary, the kind of men you might pass in a street without a second thought. Yet their eyes held that same cold discipline, that same trained stillness, and their skin shined gold.

They both looked up at me, and one of them gave a scoff, as if my presence offended him.

They appeared to be around my age, if age still meant anything. Their faces were young enough, their bodies strong, but I carried thousands of years in my bones that were no longer bones, and in a mind that could not stop counting the impossible distance between who I had been and what I was now.

"I'll leave you alone," Elit announced. "Meet your new sergeant."

He turned and walked out without another word. The doors sealed behind him with a soft, final hush, and the room seemed to grow quieter the moment he was gone. Only the low rumble of the ship remained, steady as a distant drum.

It came as a surprise even to me.

I never wanted this. I never asked to be a sergeant, never asked to lead anyone, and I certainly never asked to fight another battle in a world that was not mine. I did not even have a heart for it, not in the way a man should. My body could not swell with courage or drop with fear. It only moved.

The two men stayed seated at the round table, their bodies still, their eyes on me. Their faces carried the same hard discipline I had felt from them in the facility.

I stepped closer.

They did not rise.

I stopped at the edge of the table and, out of habit, out of old manners, extended my hand as a greeting.

Neither of them moved.

They only stared at my open palm as if it were an insult.

Slowly, I lowered it.

One of the men let out a short breath through his nose, half a laugh, half contempt. Then he leaned back in his chair, eyes narrowed.

"What makes you think you can walk in here and call yourself our sergeant?" he asked.

The challenge in his voice, and the rudeness of it, struck something stubborn in me. If they meant to break me, they would find I did not bend easily.

I straightened my back and held my ground. I would not lose my posture to a hostile lout. I would not let him see me waver.

Whatever I am now, I'm all in.

"If they chose me to be your sergeant," I said, "then you clearly lack what it takes to lead. You've been here longer than I have, and still they chose me. That must be a bitter thing to swallow."

"Swallow?" he snapped. "What the hell are you talking about?"

"Do not speak of hell before me," I said, my voice turning hard, "or I will send you there."

His expression flickered. The anger remained, but something else stirred beneath it.

"Hell?" he repeated. "What is hell, anyway?"

Across the table, the other man had not made a sound. He had sat like stone the entire time, eyes watching, face unreadable.

Now he leaned forward slightly, drawn in despite himself, and asked in a low, careful voice, "What is hell?"

I stared at them. "You don't know?"

The first man leaned back, eyes narrowed. He looked furious, yet curious all at once, like a boy scowling through a lesson he did not want but could not stop listening to.

"It is where sinners go when they die," I said.

My voice sounded steadier than my thoughts.

"A place of punishment. Fire and brimstone. Smoke so thick it chokes the soul. A world ruled by Satan, far from God and farther still from mercy."

I looked from one man to the other, measuring their faces, wondering if any of it reached them.

"In hell," I continued, "you are not granted rest. You are tormented without end. Not only by flame, but by the weight of what you have done. Your wrongs follow you there like chains. Your transgressions are made into a prison, and every hour is the same as the last."

I swallowed, though my body did not need it.

"God alone may judge you when you fall in battle," I said. "But you will go there all the same."

For the first time, both men looked uneasy.

The one who had been sneering a moment ago went still, the scoff dying in his throat. The other leaned back a fraction, eyes widening as if he had just realized the words were not a story meant to entertain, but a warning.

They did not laugh.

They looked frightened.

"We're not permitted to speak of what happens after we die," he said, voice lower now. "We were taught that Emerald One will revive us. That we will live forever in peace."

He swallowed, his eyes flicking to the other man, as if checking whether he should have said even that.

"If we fall in battle," he continued, "they take us back. And later…they revive us."

"Revive?" I said. "We have no flesh to mend. We are only a yolk sealed inside an eggshell. Break the shell, and the yolk spills with it. What is there to bring back?"

I kept my voice calm, though my thoughts pressed hard.

I lifted a hand and tapped the side of my head.

"Here, there is only one place that truly matters," I said. "The brain."

The two men watched me more closely now.

"You saw what happened with Elit," I continued. "I brought him back."

Their eyes widened at the reminder, and for the first time the scoffing man looked uncertain.

"But his injury was to his body," I said. "The shell. The vessel. The thing that can be repaired."

I held their gaze.

"If a shot destroys what sits inside," I said quietly, "if it ruins the mind itself, then tell me this. What does Emerald One revive?"

The doors swung open.

Both men straightened at once, chairs scraping softly as they sat upright. Whatever had been in their faces a moment ago vanished, replaced by rigid stillness. Their eyes dropped to the table, then flicked forward, guilty in a way that needed no explanation.

I turned.

The woman stood in the doorway, calm and unhurried, as if she had been there all along. Dark hair, sun-browned skin, and a gaze that did not raise its voice yet somehow filled the room.

"I am your captain," she said. "Alma."

The room went silent.

I looked back at her, meeting her eyes. She held my gaze for a moment longer than necessary, long enough for me to know the interruption had not been accidental.

Then she stepped forward, and the moment was over.

"It's a pleasure to meet you, Gregory," she said. "I've heard a great deal about you."

She gestured lightly to the room, as if the ship itself were an extension of her will.

"Make yourself at home. This is my ship. We will arrive at our destination in approximately one week."

She paced as she spoke, every word measured.

"We adjust our speed in intervals to keep the engines cool. At present, we are at cruising speed. Later, we will enter time-speed. When that happens, all personnel will be required to be gelled. You will be notified."

She stopped and met my eyes for a brief moment.

"Until then," she said, "use the time wisely."

And with that, she turned and walked out. The doors sealed behind her with a heavy finality, leaving the room quiet once more.

"Do you think she heard us?" the soldier whispered, suddenly nervous.

"Of course she heard us," I said. "Does it matter?"

He glanced toward the sealed doors as if they might open again.

"We're still alive for one reason," I continued, keeping my voice low but steady. "They need us. So keep your nerve."

"You asked what hell was," I said. "Look around. This is it."

"Yes sergeant."

Chapter Nine

TEAM BUILDING

The lights dimmed without warning.

White swallowed the room.

The round table blinked out. The chairs vanished a breath later, and Calder and Marek dropped hard to the floor, catching themselves with quick hands.

No siren. No warning.

Only a low metallic rattle that rose through my boots as the floor reconfigured, plates locking with dull clicks, seams sealing like scars.

The walls slid outward. The ceiling lifted. The space stretched until it felt less like a room and more like a hollowed bone.

A voice filled it, flat and bodiless.

"Training simulation. Your mission: secure the ship."

Confusion overtook me, but I shook it off.

No weakness.

I turned to my new team.

"Names."

The talker straightened at once, chin high like he'd been called to attention. "Corporal Calder."

The other answered a second later, like an echo, "Private Marek."

I nodded once.

"Stack."

Calder moved immediately, taking left without waiting.

Marek drifted back a pace, rifle low but ready, eyes tracking the new area that did not exist a second ago.

My mind sharpened.

Then the white bled into color.

Steel replaced the smooth walls. Harsh lights snapped on overhead. The dome became corridors. Bulkheads. Grated floor that rang under our steps.

Definitely not our ship.

A corridor stretched ahead with narrow windows like watching eyes set into the walls. Calder held left. Marek stayed rear. I took point.

We moved.

Silent.

Then the alarm hit.

Loud. Pulsing. A deep, repeating bass that punched through the floor and into our metal bones, like the ship was trying to beat itself alive.

We pushed forward anyway.

A T-junction.

I leaned right. Clear.

Leaned left. Clear.

"Left," I said. "Toward center."

We advanced.

BZZ.

The first beam tore over our heads.

Hot enough that my shoulder plate sizzled like a frying pan.

We dropped on instinct.

Another shot struck between us and carved a glowing scar into the metal.

Not simulation fire. Not warning shots.

Kill shots.

I fired back without seeing a face. Calder fired too, disbelief, like the ship itself had turned predator.

We rose and ran, rifles sweeping the corridor.

Nothing.

No targets. No footsteps. No shadows.

Only the alarm, hammering.

Next junction.

I peeked right.

Movement. Low. Fast.

A reptilian figure, scaled and narrow, weapon already raised.

I snapped back to cover.

Calder slid his barrel around the corner and sent a burst down the corridor.

Return fire snapped past the wall, so close it hissed.

I leaned out and fired once. Clean.

The creature's head ruptured.

Dark matter and vapor that vanished too quickly, leaving a stumbling Reptilian body behind in a splash of orange.

We kept moving.

No time to stare at the impossible. No time for questions.

The corridor opened into a bay.

Wide. Very wide. Space warping wide.

Crates stacked like barricades. Catwalk above. Shadows high enough to hide armies.

Calder glanced at me. "Ready?"

"Yes."

He tossed a small sphere.

It hit the floor and bloomed into white light, brutal yet pure, washing the bay's corners clean.

"Move."

We rushed in.

Beams raked the open floor instantly. Metal screamed. Sparks leapt. The sound was constant, like angry insects chewing the air.

We slid behind a crate as fire stitched the space we'd just crossed.

I rose just enough to see.

A Reptilian soldier on the balcony, firing down.

I put a burst into its head.

It dropped out of sight.

I ducked back down.

Don't stay up. Don't be the fool who thinks courage makes you bulletproof.

That lesson was older than this body.

"Marek," I said. "Next crate. Right side. Now."

He moved before the sentence ended.

Fast. Clean.

Beams chased him, striking the floor inches from his shoulder, but he hit cover like he'd practiced this in his sleep.

"On three," I said.

Calder nodded once.

"One."

The alarm hammered.

"Two."

The ship vibrated under us.

"Three."

We rose together and fired in one rhythm, three guns speaking as one line.

Three targets dropped.

We sank back behind cover before the return fire could find us.

I shifted toward Calder's crate, crossing open ground in a low sprint.

Two shots snapped past me, close enough to burn the air.

I hit the floor beside him.

"I'm advancing," I said. "Cover."

Calder didn't answer. He didn't need to.

He laid down fire.

I ran.

Shot while moving.

Dove behind the next crate.

The beams thinned.

Calder's shots found two more enemies.

The bay stuttered into silence.

Only the alarm remained, pulsing like a deafening heartbeat.

"Next room," I said. "On my count."

We ran on three, firing as we moved, not to kill, to force heads down.

We hit the doorway and spilled through.

And the air changed.

It was cooler and the air was circulated with a loud army of fans.

The room did not contain supplies. Not weapons.

Shelves climbed the walls from floor to ceiling, rows upon rows.

Jars.

Hundreds.

Inside each jar floated something pale and folded, suspended in gel.

Human brains.

Wired into the racks with vine-like cords that pulsed faintly, feeding and draining, as if the room itself breathed through them.

For one sick second, the fight fell away.

The bay. The Reptilians. The alarms.

None of it mattered next to this.

Then beams snapped through the doorway behind us, and the spell broke.

We returned fire.

Calder moved left, taking angles like he'd been born in skirmishes.

Marek held rear and placed careful shots, each one deliberate, each one final.

The reptilian soldiers surged in, frantic and hungry, but we cut them down, driving them back until the last one fell and the doorway stayed empty.

Silence.

Not peace.

Silence like holding your breath underwater.

The alarm still pulsed somewhere beyond the walls, but in here there was only the low hum of the racks.

All three of us stepped closer.

Brains floated in thick gel. Pale. Delicate.

Some jars trembled almost imperceptibly, as if something inside still dreamed.

I caught my reflection in the glass.

Armor.

Emerald light.

A face that looked like mine only because it had been shaped to calm my mind.

Is this all we are? I thought to myself.

Calder spoke, voice stripped bare.

"Is this all we are?"

Marek stood a step back, head tilted, staring at the labels, the cords, the way the light pulsed through them.

Before anyone could say another word, the world flashed white.

The shelves vanished.

The jars vanished.

The circulating air cut out mid-breath.

The alarm died. Thank God.

The ship, the bay, the bodies, the brains, all of it erased as if it had never existed.

We stood in the original white chamber again, empty air around us, the only sound our own quiet stillness.

"Simulation complete."

I looked at Marek.

He met my eyes for a heartbeat, then looked away, as if the connection itself was dangerous.

I looked at Calder.

He gave me a small nod.

Not approval.

Acknowledgment.

As if we had just seen the truth, and the truth had seen us back.

Chapter Ten
TIME-SPEED

The white snapped away.

At first, there was nothing, just blackout, like the ship had blinked.

Then the room rebuilt itself around us.

Metal returned under my boots. The low vibration in the deck. Panels sealed into place with soft clicks. The air became still.

The table snapped back into existence.

Solid. Sudden.

The walls no longer felt endless. They felt close, armored, and alive.

A window to my left held the night of space.

Silence settled over the room as if the ship itself was waiting for the next command.

Then, behind us, in the corner of the room…

Elit sat with his hands folded, perfectly calm, like the last thirty minutes had not happened.

He clapped his hands.

The sole percussion of his hands striking in applause eerily echoed off the metal of the ship.

"Training mission complete," he said. "You did well."

He didn't smile. He didn't need to.

"We have more to cover."

He motioned to the seats. We sat.

A map flickered to life above the table, opaque at first, then sharpening into a blueprint. Corridors branched like veins. Intersections glowed. A pulsing light traced the routes we'd just walked.

Elit's gaze held on me a fraction too long.

"Our objective is to reclaim what was stolen."

He tapped the hologram. A chamber flashed.

"The jars you saw are not cargo," he said. "They are minds. Heroes. Soldiers. Our greatest thinkers. The ones who built what remains of Earth."

His voice didn't soften. It sharpened.

"During the recent attack, the Reptilians destroyed one of our research centers and took them."

He paused.

"They took our souls."

The hologram pulsed again. A narrow route appeared through the ship we just ran through.

"And we will take them back."

He leaned forward slightly, as if bringing us closer to a fire.

"You now know the layout. That is why we trained. Once you are inside, you will move like you've already lived there."

His eyes narrowed.

"Getting you aboard is the only uncertain part. The ship will identify you the moment we close distance. There will be no negotiation. There will be one chance."

The route on the map brightened, then tightened, like a noose.

"So we will not approach as soldiers."

He said it like an obvious fact.

"We will approach as debris."

A new image formed above the table. Three small ovals. Sealed capsules.

"Insertion shells," Elit said. "You will be sealed inside, suspended in pressurized gel. Impact absorption. Thermal control."

He tapped three points along the ship's outer hull.

"All three shells strike at the same moment. You breach. You move. The ship goes to full alert."

He looked at each of us without blinking.

"Our support craft withdraws the instant you launch. We remain cloaked and silent. You will have minutes, not hours."

"Do not waste them."

I stared at the map. The pulsing route. The precision.

A thought slipped in, cold and clean.

How did we catch them so fast? With that kind of head start, they should already be gone.

The doors slid open behind us.

"It's Captain Alma," Calder whispered to me.

Captain Alma stepped in with two subordinates, and the temperature of the room changed the way it changes when a blade is drawn. Calder and Marek sat straighter without thinking, like discipline had been welded into their bones.

Alma's eyes raked the hologram, then landed on us.

"Alright," she said. "Mr. Lizard and the three space debris."

No humor. No softness. Just a summary of what we truly were to her.

I stood.

"My name is Gregory."

Calder and Marek went still. The air tightened. Every gaze swung to me as if I'd spoken out of turn in church.

Alma's mouth twitched, not quite a smile. She stepped close and put her palm on my chest like she owned the space between us.

"It's been a while since someone corrected me," she said.

I didn't move.

"Remove your hand," I said. "Only my wife lays hands on me."

A short laugh escaped her, amused in the way a predator is amused by a rabbit's courage.

She turned toward the door.

"Everyone to your posts," she said. "We are entering time-speed."

Her eyes cut back to me, sharp as a hook.

"Gregory. Officer Xut will seat you."

She left with her lieutenant. The doors sealed behind them with a soft hush.

Xut remained.

Smaller than Alma. Compact. Uniform immaculate. Face blank.

"Follow me," he said.

He led me back to the room I had woken in. The bed waited in the same position, too neat, too still.

I sat on the edge.

Xut opened a cabinet and removed two thick cables. He held them like restraints.

"Arms," he said. "Palms up."

I lifted my arms.

As the cable ends neared my wrists, my skin parted on its own.

A clean circle opened in my synthetic flesh. Inside: hollow, intricate, metallic geometry. Green lightning flickering like a trapped storm.

Xut snapped the first cable into place.

Hard click.

Soft hiss as the seal took.

He did the other wrist.

The green light steadied. Began to pulse.

Beneath it, the faint gold glow in my arms answered, syncing with it, like my body was learning a new heartbeat.

"Lie back," Xut said.

I lowered myself onto the bed.

He pressed a button on the wall.

A lid slid from the bedframe, transparent and curved, and folded over me in one smooth motion until it sealed shut.

A glass coffin.

Beautiful in the way a weapon is beautiful.

"Good night," Xut said.

The chamber began to fill.

Gel poured in.

Red. Dense.

The color of crushed fruit and fresh blood.

It rose fast.

My shoulders disappeared.

My throat.

My mouth.

Pressure closed in from every side, slow and absolute, until I floated off the mattress, suspended in the center of the coffin.

The gel pinned me without touching bone.

It pressed into every seam of me.

Packed.

Contained.

A memory flashed.

Panic.

Darkness.

Soil against my lashes.

Grit in my teeth.

No air.

My mind tried to climb away from it.

The world was muffled.

Close.

Airless.

And then, as if the future wanted to teach me a lesson in the language I understood best…

Silence.

Chapter Eleven
LAZARUS

Alone with my thoughts.

The gel pressed in from every side, heavy as earth. It stole the last illusion of air. With nothing to see, the past came into my vision. It always did.

My wife on the porch. Snow gathering on the rail. Quilt pulled tight. Her stare fixed on the distance. A stare that only comes when you're deep in thought.

I wondered what she was thinking. Not grand things. Not dreams. But *real* heavy weighted worries. The next meal. The next log. Whether our son had eaten. Whether our daughter was ill. Whether the roof would hold under the weight of the snow.

She had been pinned long before I ever was.

Not by chains.

Not by a draft to war.

By need. By motherhood. By poverty.

Time had no edges in the coffin. No light to count. No sound but the dull lie of stillness.

Then the gel vanished with a wet pull, like the chamber had lost interest in holding me.

I dropped toward the bed. The lid peeled open with a hiss.

I sat up too fast, panic erecting my body out of the bed to freedom. I was like a fly finding an open window.

I yanked the cables from my wrists. One. Then the other.

I stood and crossed to the window.

Stars.

Cold. Endless.

Indifferent.

A speaker crackled overhead.

"Your presence is requested in the meeting room. Please report promptly. Repeat. Your presence is requested in the meeting room."

Of course.

They never let the silence last.

The door sensed me and slid open.

Across the hall, Calder stepped out of his room at the same time. He met my eyes and held them. Not friendly. Not hostile. Just the look of a man who's been through something and doesn't know what it made him.

"Morning, Lazarus," I said. "Did you hop out of the grave too?"

He blinked once, then gave a quiet, reluctant laugh.

"Lazarus? I'm Calder."

"No kidding." I glanced at my wrists. "Next time, I'm requesting cremation."

That got a real laugh.

"Cremation," Calder muttered. "Luxury. They'll toss us in the bargain bin. Two-for-one. No lid, no prayers, and they'll charge us for the smoke."

I smiled, then caught on a word.

"Prayers?" I said. "Last time we spoke, you didn't even know hell existed."

Calder's smile died.

He glanced down the corridor, then back at me. His voice dropped until it was barely breath.

"Walk," he said. "Not here."

We fell into step, side by side. The ship rumbled around us. Oval windows slid past like watching eyes.

Calder kept his gaze forward.

"I have something," he murmured. "A device. Forbidden."

I didn't prompt him. I just waited.

"I took it on a raid," he said. "Outpost. We cleared rooms, seized what we were told to seize, burned the rest." His hand drifted toward his side, checking without looking. "It doesn't talk unless you ask it. No voice. No prompts. You type."

I glanced at him. "And you typed 'hell'."

Calder swallowed.

"Before they sealed me," he said, "I searched one word."

He hesitated, like saying it out loud might make it real.

"Hell."

He didn't look at me when he added, "It answered."

The corridor turned.

We rounded the corner and nearly collided with Marek.

He stepped back, startled, then recovered too quickly, eyes doing their quiet measuring.

"Sorry," Marek said. Then he frowned, caught on something. "What… answered?"

Calder's posture tightened.

"You," Calder snapped. "I told you to stand down. You said 'yes sir'."

Marek's brow furrowed. He glanced between us, still confused, still listening.

"I only caught the end," he said. "That's all."

I stepped in fast.

"And that's all there was," I said. "Meeting room. We're already late."

Marek hesitated, then fell in with us.

But the word stayed alive behind his eyes.

Answered.

Suspicion didn't need much room to grow.

The meeting-room doors slid open.

Elit. Alma. Xut. Another lieutenant I hadn't met yet. All seated around the round table, heads bent toward a rotating hologram.

A ship rendered in pale light. Corridors branching like veins. Breach points pulsing. Routes glowing.

None of them looked up at first.

Their voices were quiet fragments, stiff and confident. The words they used were to impress one another more than communicate a plan. Aye. Big Whigs. They are the same in every generation.

They are the brains.

We are the implements.

"Sit," Elit said at last, without lifting his eyes. "We have much to discuss."

We took our seats across from them.

Elit lifted a hand and the hologram tightened, focusing on three bright points along the hull.

"This is your insertion," he said. "You will strike here, here, and here. You trained on the layout. You will move room to room exactly as rehearsed. You will not…"

The doors slid open.

A figure entered without pause, without announcement, like the room belonged to him and we were the ones intruding.

The air changed.

Even Alma stiffened. Calder and Marek sat straighter without thinking.

Elit cut off mid-sentence.

The newcomer's gaze swept the room once and settled on me.

He walked to my side of the table.

Instinct rose. I stood.

He extended a hand.

It looked human until you noticed the glow.

"Brigadier General Voss," he said.

I took his hand out of habit. Tried to give him the firm shake my father taught me.

His palm was cool. His grip controlled. As if crushing my fingers would require effort and he simply didn't bother.

Voss held my gaze too long.

"It's a pleasure," he said, "to meet a true soldier."

His eyes didn't soften.

"One who fought the enemy *and* the ailments of flesh."

He released my hand and turned back to the hologram like the introduction was an afterthought.

"Now," he said, "we discuss what happens after you clear the ship."

Elit leaned forward, a thin edge of irritation slipping into his tone.

"We must go over the details," Elit said. "Protocols. Timelines. Rules of engagement."

Voss didn't look at him.

"No need," he said.

Simple.

Final.

Elit grunted.

Voss angled his head just enough to acknowledge him, the smallest tilt of authority.

"I watched their training," he said. Then his eyes flicked to me. "I watched him."

My spine went cold in a place I no longer had nerves.

"Let his instincts do the work," Voss said. "That is what you brought him here for."

His finger traced the hologram to the chamber marked with the densest cluster of symbols.

"Once you secure the brain room," Voss said, "my forces will follow and sanitize the ship."

Silence dropped.

Elit's mouth parted, but nothing came out.

Voss didn't wait for permission.

He turned from the table as if the matter was settled.

He walked out.

The doors sealed behind him.

The silence he left felt heavier than the ship's hull.

I looked around the table.

No one spoke.

No one met my eyes.

"When do we begin?" I asked.

Chapter Twelve

INSERTION SHELLS

Deep within the ship, on its lowest level near the rear, lay a vast launch chamber. The ceiling arched high above us, swallowing sound. Along the outer wall, tunnels ran straight into the black of space, each one a long iron throat sealed by a thick window like a ship's looking glass.

From inside the chamber the exits looked small, not because they were narrow, but because the room was enormous.

Crews navigated the dock like second nature. Everyone had their role, and everyone did it well.

Machines hovered and extended lightning arms beneath the insertion shells, lifting them with a gentle buzz. Blue lightning webbed from machine to pod, careful and intimate, like a mother cradling an infant.

There were twelve insertion shells in all, lined up like pale eggs waiting to be thrown.

Our plan was straightforward, brutal, timed to the breath.

All twelve would launch at once. They would strike in groups of three, hitting different sections of the target ship to fracture its response and scatter its attention. Two shells in each set carried charges meant to tear open corridors and doors. The third carried a localized pulse designed to blind sensors and disrupt systems long enough for confusion to blind the enemy.

A rainbow of surprises, Elit had called it.

The breaches made by the other shells would not be wasted. They were for Voss's troops, who would follow once the brain room was secured, pouring through the openings to sanitize whatever we left unfinished.

This mission could turn delicate in an instant. If the Reptilians realized they were losing the ship, they might destroy the brains in spite. In this case, we would win the battle and gain nothing. Worse than nothing. We would leave those minds snuffed out inside their glass prisons.

I took it personally anyway.

Not because I believed Elit's speeches. Not because Voss's certainty had infected me. But because I knew what it was to be reduced to a number. To be treated like cargo. To be buried while still breathing.

Those brains in the jars were alive, trapped in blind darkness, listening to the world move without them.

Hell.

The word came easily now. Too easily. I turned it over without hesitation, as if the world had ground hope down through unanswered prayers and misfortune until only blunt language remained.

Maybe that was the corruption of this place.

Or maybe it was honesty at last.

Still, my thoughts betrayed me. I thought of Job, of suffering that was not punishment but trial. Of faith tested until it either broke, or hardened into something unrecognizable.

Was this another test?

"Positions," I said sharply to Calder and Marek.

They moved at once, brisk and disciplined, jogging toward their assigned shells.

Calder glanced back over his shoulder. In the green glow of the chamber, his attempt at humor looked almost brave.

"I've done the cocoon," he called. "I expect the butterfly."

Then he disappeared into his pod.

Marek said nothing. He only climbed into his shell with the calm of a man stepping into a coffin he had already accepted.

I climbed into mine.

The glass lid snapped shut in the blink of an eye, sealing me away from the chamber, from the ambient drone, from the voices. Silence poured in like water. For a moment I lay still with my eyes closed and listened to nothing at all.

Then, without warning, I felt it.

A tremor in my limbs. A tightening in my chest area. Nerves. A rush. Fear finding a place to live inside this machine.

The weight of what I was about to do struck harder than it had in the meeting room.

My mind swarmed with hostile thoughts.

What if I die on impact. What if this is a trap. What if they take me prisoner and keep me awake in the dark, in a jar for eternity.

There was no release for it. No one to speak to. No room to pace. I was sealed in my own silence, and I was the one they expected to be a leader.

I could show no weakness.

A faint hiss sounded, and the gel began to rise.

The same thick gel as before, heavy as packed earth. It climbed along my sides and over my ribs, pressing against me from the outside and seeming to press from within, too, as if it wanted to erase the last small space I could call my own.

A voice clicked into my ear, crisp and controlled.

"Team, this is Elit," it said. "We are monitoring from the meeting room and will provide intel as it becomes available."

A pause, then the sound of distant instruments, faint and steady.

"The target ship is on our scope. We are waiting for the optimal launch window. Once the lock is confirmed, you will receive a ten-second countdown. Brace accordingly."

His tone did not change.

"The ride will be less gentle than your quarters."

Another pause.

"Good luck. The future of a thousand souls is in your hands. Elit out."

Anticipation swelled until it felt like pressure beneath my skin.

I was locked in place. Not even a twitch was possible. The gel held me the way the earth once had, firm and indifferent. I could not help wondering what was moving through Calder's mind, or Marek's. What did a man think about when he believed he might be seconds from ending?

I knew almost nothing about them. Only that we were bound together now, three lives on the same thread, and that thread was about to be pulled tight.

Back home, we had marched through snow and cold until our feet went numb and the world became white misery.

This was worse.

This was marching through the depths of the mind, where snow and cold could not compete.

A voice returned in my ear, flat and mechanical.

"Ten."

"Nine."

"Eight."

"Seven."

"Six."

"Five."

"Four."

My thoughts broke into prayer.

Lord…

"Three."

This is in…

"Two."

Your…

"One."

Hands.

The pod jerked violently as the gel shifted, slamming backward. My stomach did not drop, but something in my mind did. The shell launched.

I could see nothing. The gel turned the world into blindness. There was only motion I could not measure, and time that refused to be read. I was stuck here, suspended and helpless, at the mercy of whatever waited beyond the hull.

When we hit, I'm supposed to stand.

To fight.

To lead.

A whole mission waited on the other side, and merely reaching it already felt like more than any man should be asked to endure.

Though I was nothing but a brain, it still yearned to be free.

Confined in a skull or confined in iron, the mind still clawed for open air. Yet a brain did not know sunlight. It knew only the dark behind the eyes.

It was the soul that craved the light.

I prayed to climb out of this grave once more.

"Brace for impact," Elit warned in my ear.

The world became violence.

A crash like the sky splitting. The pod slammed through metal and I was thrown forward into the nose of the shell. My legs folded until I slammed against the nose of the pod beneath me. My vision stuttered, glitching in hard frames, as if even my eyes needed a moment to remember how to see.

Before I could even draw a breath of relief, the gel slurped away from my body, retreating with a wet hiss. The glass visor blew outward and vanished into the corridor.

I sprang out, seized my weapon, and snapped it to my shoulder. I checked my surroundings the only way I could. Left. Right. Behind. Above. A full sweep, fast and frantic.

Two more impacts thundered almost at once.

Crash.

Crash.

The other shells punched through the hull on my left and right, so close I felt the heat of their passage. For a heartbeat I thought they would clip me and smear me across the corridor.

Their visors ejected. Calder and Marek vaulted out the same way I had, weapons up, movements clean.

"Entry point is clear," I said. "Move."

We advanced down the corridor in a tight line, our footfalls ringing off the metal floor. The air smelled toxic, sharp and burnt. We reached a junction.

I checked right. Calder checked left.

Clear.

We took the left passage.

Something felt off almost immediately. Not danger.

Absence.

The corridor was too quiet, too empty. We reached another junction and turned right.

Still nothing.

"Hold," I said, raising my hand.

Calder slowed beside me. "What is this?"

I stared at the floor.

"Blood," I said. "*Red* blood."

Human.

It was smeared along the wall in long strokes, pooled in corners, tracked in footprints that did not belong to us. Wires hung from torn panels and sparked in quick bursts. Lights strobed overhead, broken and irregular.

But there was no alarm.

No pulse of warning. No siren. No automated voice.

Only the ship's low tremor.

"Keep moving," Elit said in my ear. "Stick to the mission."

I did not answer.

We advanced again, slower now, weapons sweeping. The deeper we went, the worse it looked. Damage, scorch marks, ripped access plates, as if someone had already fought their way through. As if the ship had been opened and stripped.

"Gregory," Elit said, sharper. "Keep moving. That is an order."

I looked at Calder. He looked back at me, and I saw the same thought in his eyes.

This was not what we trained for.

We reached the crate storage chamber, the place where the simulation had nearly drowned us in fire.

In training it had been chaos.

Here it was quiet enough to hear the zapping of the cut wires.

No bodies. No movement. No sound.

Just blood.

The room looked ransacked, as if someone had searched for something in a hurry and left angry about what they did not find. The damaged lights strobed working hard to stay lit.

Is this a trap?

A beam of light cut through the air and kissed my cheek. Heat flashed across my face, sharp enough to sting even through the suit.

We hit the ground hard as one.

Prone, we crawled for cover, metal scraping softly against the floor. The strobing lights made the room jump in broken flashes, bright, dark, bright again, as if the ship itself were blinking.

A second beam lanced through the chamber and punched straight through the crate between Marek and me. The metal around the hole glowed white for a heartbeat, then dripped.

It was now or never.

I launched myself to the next crate. The shot chased me, scorching the floor where my legs had been an instant before. Heat ghosted across my back like a hand.

Calder and Marek rose at the same time and returned fire. Their beams hit together, and whatever had fired at us burst into wet fragments against the far wall.

The room fell silent again.

No footsteps. No alarms. No answering shots.

Just the ship's hum, and the faint hiss of something cooling where it had been melted.

I lifted my hand and signaled forward.

We advanced in a tight, deliberate line, moving slow and meticulous, weapons sweeping, every angle checked twice.

Ahead, the corridor narrowed into the passage that would lead us toward the brain room.

And the silence followed us there.

As we found the mouth of the corridor, Marek drifted to the rear, watching our six.

"Wait," he said.

We froze.

He pointed with the tip of his weapon. Between two crates, half hidden in the strobing light, a body lay sprawled facedown on the deck.

A Reptilian.

Dead.

I stared at it for a beat too long. In training, they had come at us in waves. Here, one lay already finished, as if the fight had happened without us.

"That's not our kill," I said. "Cover me."

Calder shifted his stance to give me an angle. Marek held rear security, rigid and silent.

I moved in slow, crouched steps and knelt beside the body.

Up close, the details turned my stomach. The hide was split in small, clean punctures. Not scorching. Not melted. No blackened edges.

I touched one mark with the tip of my armored hand.

Holes.

Round, punched through.

Bullet wounds.

"This wasn't done with a beam," I muttered. "These are bullets."

I looked up at Calder and Marek.

"And I know these wounds," I added. "Someone fired old lead in here."

"Don't shoot!" a voice cried from down the corridor.

All three of us whipped around, weapons up, sights trained on the dark corridor.

A figure limped into view, hands raised, breath ragged.

"What?" Calder blurted. "A Human of Flesh?"

"Please," the stranger gasped. "Help me."

I fired without hesitation.

The shot took his head in a wet flash. Orange sprayed the wall beside him. What was left of him collapsed, shuddered, and sagged into its true shape.

A Reptilian.

Marek stared, then snapped his gaze to me. "How did you know?"

I kept my weapon trained on the body until it stopped moving.

"He walked over that sharp metal grate barefoot," I said. "No shoes."

I nodded at the ribbed flooring under our feet.

"No flesh man could do that without a wince," I added. "He walked too casually, with no visual of pain."

Calder's face tightened, whatever hope had risen in him dying just as quickly.

"Move," I said.

We worked our way back into the corridor, tighter now, quieter now. We were close to the brain room.

There had to be more.

We approached a heavily armored door, the brain room on the other side.

We took positions.

I held the right side of the frame. Calder took the left. Marek crouched between us and pressed a small charge against the lock housing, fingers steady and precise.

Calder drew one of his lightning balls, a flash charge meant to blind and stun, and palmed it tight. His thumb braced on the release as if he were holding a live coal.

We were perfectly still with anticipation. Three men, one door, one breath.

"On one," I whispered. "Three…"

We never made it to even two.

The door detonated from the inside.

Metal screamed. Fragments burst outward like shrapnel, slamming into our armor and hurling all three of us backward. I hit the wall behind with enough force to rattle my iron skull, the impact ringing through my frame like a bell.

Calder's flash charge flew from his hand and struck the deck at our feet.

It triggered.

White light erupted, violent and immediate, flooding the corridor. For an instant the world became nothing but brightness. My vision vanished. All I saw was blank.

We were blind.

Through the whiteout, I heard movement beyond the ruined doorway, fast and light, scurrying to positions.

"Stay low!" I shouted.

Snow had taught me this. White pain. Burning light. Men firing blind. You did not run. You went low and let death pass over you.

We laid prone. Blinking frantically.

With a sudden rawer, beams tore through the doorway above us, carving bright scars into the wall where our heads would have been. The corridor rang with each impact. The room was thick with smoke and fumigated with the toxic smell of melted metal.

My vision crawled back in slow pieces. Shapes first. Then edges. Then the doorway itself.

The door had been nearly nine feet tall. The blast had torn away the upper two-thirds, but the bottom three feet remained,

Calder stood frozen over the smoking muzzle.

Then his suit lights flickered.

Once.

Twice.

Like a warning trying to decide whether mercy existed.

Gone.

Calder's body dropped like dead weight, armor clanking as it hit the deck.

My hands locked.

Not by choice.

Not by fear.

Something took them.

The edges of my vision dimmed. The world narrowed into a tunnel, the strobing lights stretching into long, sick streaks.

My body fell towards the ground.

"Hens…" I tried to speak, but the word didn't form. My mouth didn't cooperate.

My ears filled with a rising tone, thin and sharp, like a blade being drawn.

And under it, faintly, through the rush.

Elit's voice again.

Crackling in and out as his voice stretched and slowed like a dying music box.

"Sanitation protocol initiated. Back up requested immediately."

The words barely landed before the world tipped.

Blackness poured in.

And I fell into it.

Chapter Thirteen
Reborn

Consciousness was faint, more dream than waking. True darkness. Life in its smallest form, reduced to thought, and then to soul.

I clawed for life.

There was nothing to grab. No hands to fold in prayer. I was stranded at sea with no shore on any horizon, only the weight of black water and the certainty that I was sinking.

In the distance, a white light appeared.

I tried to pull away, but the light pulled back. It widened, reaching for me as if it had hands of its own. I fought with everything I had. There were no words in that place, only flashes of vision, fragments without sound. I kept tearing myself backward, refusing it, refusing the clean, bright emptiness it promised.

Then I felt it.

Behind me, a green glow.

I reached for it with all my strength. The harder I reached, the brighter it burned, as if it recognized me. The green swelled until it filled the darkness, until it was no longer a glow but a gathering storm.

It cracked into lightning.

The world vibrated with a deafening buzz. The green pulsed, tightened, and suddenly condensed into a single point of force. It flared into a red-white burst, then snapped back into shape again, like a net drawn in.

It caught me.

It dragged me through the dark like a hook through water.

Then it released me.

My head broke the surface. Air hit me hard. My eyes snapped open.

A rifle barrel hovered inches from my face.

Brigadier General Voss stood over me, posture loose, as if waking prisoners was a chore on his list. An arrogant smile rested on his mouth like it belonged there.

"Housekeeping," he said.

His finger tightened.

A crack answered from behind him.

Voss's head erupted in red mist and heat. The spray turned to steam midair.

His body swayed, confused without command, and collapsed with a heavy metallic thud.

At the jagged breach, Captain Hensley stood braced in the opening, both hands locked on my scorched rifle he should not have had. The muzzle glowed, smoking.

He did not speak. He only tossed the rifle through the breach back to me.

I caught it on instinct.

And I moved.

No hesitation.

Two men came sprinting around the corner, drawn by the blast. I met them with the rifle before they could even lift their weapons.

The first shot took one clean in the head. The second hit the other in the chest. Sparks erupted. Wiring and circuitry burst outward like torn roots.

He staggered but did not fall right away. His body tried to keep going on failing systems, twitching with useless commands.

I went over to him, dropped to one knee, grabbed the front of his armor, and hauled his face close to mine.

"Tell me, how…" I started to say.

Then I stopped.

There was no time for questions.

I shot his head off.

Blood spattered my armor and steamed where it landed.

His body went still, and it felt lighter in my grip.

I stared at the mess.

I would not do that again at such close range.

Too messy.

I dropped the body and ran over to where Marek lay.

I tore a charge from Marek's dead frame, yanking it free from his armor plating, and slapped it onto the wall beside the hole where the captives were sealed in.

"Stand back!" I shouted, sweeping my aim down the corridor and checking our angles.

The charge detonated.

Metal screamed. The wall burst outward in shards, throwing dust and fragments across the deck. Heat rolled through the corridor.

And then they were there.

Hensley and his crew stumbled through the breach. Bloodied. Bruised. Limbs shaking with exhaustion. Skin torn and dirty, not polished metal. Real faces. Real eyes.

Humans of Flesh.

I quickly knelt down, traced the sign of the cross on Calder's forehead, and ripped his weapon out of his locked hands. I tossed it to Hensley.

I rose and faced the crew.

"We're taking Calder with us," I said. "I do not care what state he's in when we move him. If his body fails, we preserve the mind. But he does not die here. Understand?"

I let my gaze sweep across them, daring anyone to argue.

"Tell me you understand."

"Yes," Captain Hensley said at once. "You have my word."

He turned to his people. "Michael, Raza, Lee. Get those weapons." He pointed to the scattered mix of corpses still clutching their weapons laying lifelessly on the deck.

"This ship is crawling with Voss's men," I said, keeping my head on a swivel as I scanned the corridors. "I do not know how many are aboard. Our only option may be to abandon ship."

Hensley's eyes narrowed, thinking fast. "If we can reach the lower bay, there are escape pods."

He hesitated. Just a breath.

"The only problem is what comes after. Once we launch, we may have nowhere to go."

"We've been living on this ship for years," Raza said. Her voice was steady, but her hands shook as she gathered a rifle from the floor. "Let's just say we're not welcome back where we came from."

"New Jersey?" I asked before I could stop myself. "Earth?"

"Neither," Michael said.

Hensley nodded toward the corridor that led deeper into the ship. "There's a stretcher in the brain room, just through those doors. If we get in there, we can move Calder out in one piece."

"Let's move," I said.

The five of us stacked around the door to the brain room. Lights flickered. Time tightened. Four hearts were racing. Not mine.

I was responsible for all of them now.

"I go first," I said. "I check high and right. Michael, you take left the moment we enter. Hensley, follow and get us to the stretcher. Raza and Lee, watch the rear."

They nodded, quick and tense.

"Move," I ordered.

I lunged through the doorway, clearing the three-foot remnant of the door in a single bound, with Michael right behind me. I swept the room in one fast arc, eyes up first, then right.

"Clear, right," I called.

A shot cracked from my left.

Michael fired.

I snapped toward the sound just as a beam scorched past my left arm, close enough to discolor my armor's sheen. Michael's shot went wide.

I locked on to his target and dropped it with one clean burst.

I had overestimated my new team.

I suppose I'm their keeper now.

"Let's go!" I shouted.

The rest of the team poured in after us, clumsy and rushed, stumbling over the door remnants. Their weapons swung in every direction, frantic and unfocused, like swatting at flies.

Is that what I looked like when I was still flesh?

My machine body moved with clean precision. Full range of motion. No fatigue. No pain. No thirst. No sleep.

No trembling hands. No lungs tightening for air. No cramp in the calf, no stitch in the ribs, no ache in the shoulder from holding a weapon too long. My joints did not complain. My muscles did not burn. I could run until the stars went out and never slow.

I had to remember they were carrying more than I was. Fear in their bellies. Blood in their veins. A heartbeat that could betray them at any second.

"Over there," Hensley said, pointing. "Through that door. That's where we keep the stretchers."

We started toward it.

The ship lurched.

The deck dropped out from under us and threw us hard to the floor. Lights flickered in violent pulses, then snapped to full brightness.

Hensley's face tightened. "They just overrode my emergency power lock," he said. "They have full control of the ship now." His eyes darted down the corridor. "They may even have access to the motion sensors in security. They'll know exactly where we are, and exactly where we're going."

We got up and ran.

The storage room door opened as Hensley's hand hit the scanner, and we spilled inside. Rows of equipment clung to the walls. Lee hurried to a stretcher mounted vertically in a locking frame and slapped a button on its side.

It released with a soft thunk, drifted down like an autumn leaf, and then steadied, floating waist height above the deck like a quiet ghost.

"Let's get your friend," Lee said, voice tight, "and get out of here."

We rushed back toward the brain room, the stretcher gliding after us on its own, soundless.

I reached the broken doorway first. I leaned out to check the corridor to the right, then snapped back so fast my shoulder struck the frame.

A voice spoke from the hall, metallic and calm.

"Come out. Drop your weapons. You have no way out."

On the last word, something launched.

A mechanical dog cleared the three-foot remnant of the door in a single springing leap, body folding and unfolding like a weapon. It flew straight at my throat.

I raised my rifle and fired.

The dog exploded into metal fragments and sparks, skittering across the floor.

Then the hallway answered with thunder.

Not one set of footsteps.

Many.

Heavy, synchronized, closing fast.

"Spread out," I shouted "Circle. Now."

They poured in like a flood.

Dogs vaulted the broken doorway, one after another, jaws open, eyes glowing. We fired through the breach, shots lighting the room, metal bursting, bodies falling. But they kept coming. Faster. More. Relentless.

They hit the room and did not charge straight at us.

They ran around us.

Circling.

Herding.

And then blue lightning snapped into place.

It wrapped the air like a net.

My muscles locked. My fingers froze on the rifle. The others stiffened mid-breath, eyes wide, trapped in their own bodies the way I had been the first time I met these cursed things.

More dogs spilled into the room, filling every corner.

Five of them stepped into the blue field without hesitation, immune to it. They tore our weapons from our hands with efficient, practiced motions. They forced our arms behind our backs.

A condensed band of blue light tightened around our wrists, binding us like rope.

One dog sprinted to the center and stopped, posture rigid, head lifted as if it were addressing a courtroom.

Its voice buzzed cold and clean.

"You have violated several laws of the Order of the Earth. You are in our custody. Follow and obey. Acts of non-compliance will be met with deadly force."

The pack shifted formation, flowing into a horseshoe around us, leaving the doorway open like a command.

We were herded like sheep.

We made our way to the doorway, and a few of the dogs ran ahead. They moved as one, like a single living organism, arranging themselves into a staircase of metal backs and rigid limbs, stepping up and over the broken remnant of the door.

We crossed as they commanded.

We walked on, prisoners of an unknown fate.

As if slowness could bargain for time, our feet dragged. No one spoke. Even breath felt too loud. The corridor seemed longer than it had on the way in, lit in pulses that made every shadow jump.

At the end of it waited the cargo bay.

The cargo bay doors slid open.

A wall of soldiers filled the room. Fifty at least, stacked in disciplined rows. The front rank knelt. The second stood behind them, rifles leveled. The shape of a volley.

Hensley's crew gasped at the sight of such s threatening force.

My mind did not race. It hardened.

"AT EASE!" a familiar voice snapped.

The line obeyed in one clean motion. Rifles lowered. Knees rose.

Alma stepped forward. The soldiers parted for her without being told.

"I like the new color," she said. "Red. It suits you."

She placed her hand on my chest, right over the glow beneath the armor.

The pulse under my plating answered her touch. Once. Slow. Deliberate. Like it had been recognized.

I looked down for the first time since the fighting stopped.

The light beneath my armor was no longer green.

It pulsed red.

"This situation has escalated beyond its original scope," Alma said. Calm. Administrative.

"You made a decision."

"I did," I said.

She held my gaze, weighing me the way a clerk weighs a coin.

"You reached the brain room. You prevented further loss."

Then she gestured toward the far end of the bay.

"Escape pods are still operational," she said. "You and the civilians will take one."

An afterthought, sharpened into order.

"And take your wounded."

A stretcher hovered nearby, already prepared. Calder lay strapped to it, suit dark, face blank, packaged for transport.

Alma's eyes flicked from me to Calder, then back. Taking inventory.

"If you are so interested in hell," she said, the edge of a grim smile forming, "then go find it."

Hensley swallowed. "You're letting us go?"

Alma did not look at him. Her attention stayed on me.

"Your presence here serves no further purpose," she said.

Too easy.

Alma stepped closer and lowered her voice.

"Sergeant Gregory," she said, as if tasting the title. "History will decide if you were right."

Then she stepped back.

"Go," she said.

And the path was clear.

She held my gaze.

And I held hers, as if reading her intentions through her eyes.

Chapter Fourteen
Escape Pod

The escape pod was roughly ten feet by sixteen, cramped but orderly, with seats bolted along the perimeter and a small round table anchored near the rear. Up front were two seats like a carriage bench, facing a wide set of windows.

Beneath the glass, a panel of controls stretched in a shallow arc. Buttons glowed like stained glass in a church. Some blinked. Some held steady. Others stayed dark, as if waiting to be chosen.

Captain Hensley climbed into the left seat and took the controls. Michael dropped in beside him and immediately went to work, fingers moving fast over the lit panel, tapping sequences, waking systems that hummed to life beneath our feet.

We felt free, but the feeling was thin. The ship had let us go, and that made it worse. It felt like our escape came too easy, like we were walking into a trap.

The small pod lurched up, and then we shot back the moment we cleared the gate.

Silence swallowed us.

Straps tightened across chests. Metal creaked. Somewhere behind the walls, something vibrated with a low, steady thrum. This was a much bumpier ride than the other crafts I was on.

After some time, the shaking eased. The pod steadied and found a smooth line through space. Hensley kept his eyes forward.

Michael didn't stop moving, as if he paused, the whole thing would die.

In the back corner, Calder lay on the stretcher like an abandoned weapon. Lifeless. Dark. The green light that used to pulse beneath his armor was gone.

I unstrapped myself and stood. The pod felt too small when I moved. Raza and Lee rose with me, careful with their steps, as if a sudden shift might toss us all back into the walls.

I walked to Calder and stood over him.

"What do you think?" I asked.

Raza leaned in close, studying the head and neck region where the suit's encasement supported the mind. She didn't touch him yet. She watched, listening, as if the armor might whisper the truth.

"It's hard to tell," she said. "Give me a second. I need the kit."

"Kit?" I asked, the word catching in my mouth. "First aid? He doesn't have a body."

Raza glanced at me like I had asked if water was wet. "Of course. Ships carry two. Flesh and mechanical. Standard."

Lee crossed to a cabinet near the rear wall and opened it. The moment the door swung wide, the cabinet came alive. Lights bloomed along its inner frame. Instruments lifted slightly from their cradles as if waking. This was not bandages and spirits. It was a shrine of tools, delicate and intricate, each piece glowing faintly.

Lee pulled out a compact box and set it on the small table beside Calder's stretcher. The box sat there quietly, then gave a soft pulse of light, like it was eager to be used.

Raza selected a tool shaped like a knife with no blade. She thumbed a small switch at its base.

A buzz.

A blue translucent edge appeared from nothing, perfectly straight, glowing as if cut from glass. The light painted her hands, her sleeves, the underside of Calder's chin.

She lowered herself beside Calder's head and worked with reverence and speed. She cut a clean circle just above his ear. The smell hit first. Sharp. Burning. Not blood, but scorched sealant and heated alloy. A thin smoke curled up and clung to the air.

When the circle was complete, she switched to a scraping instrument and lifted the thin layer away. Beneath it was not flesh. It was golden, glowing web, with thin strands of metal wire making up a hidden interface.

She repeated the procedure on the other side.

Lee pressed a button on the box. It answered with a brighter glow and two cables unfurled, each ending in a funnel-shaped coupler. He handed one to Raza, kept the other, and they moved in unison.

They pressed the funnels against Calder's head.

Suction.

A click.

The couplers locked themselves into place.

Raza and Lee stepped back to the box and began tapping commands across its surface. The box replied in soft pulses, then a thin beep, then another.

I stood over them, doing nothing. Feeling useless. My hands were weapons. My mind was a storm. And my friend lay there with an uncertain future while other people did the saving.

Raza didn't look up as she spoke. "We're checking the status of his brain. His suit has been unpowered for hours. That's long enough to put the brain at serious risk, if he isn't already gone."

The box beeped again. Numbers crawled across a small screen. Lines rose and dipped like the tide.

Raza leaned in, eyes scanning the stream of information.

Then she exhaled.

"Okay," she said, and for the first time her voice softened. "He's still showing full function. His internal support is running on emergency reserve. Whoever shut him down didn't want him dead."

"At least not yet," Lee added, still watching the screen.

"These people are full of tricks," I said. "Who knows what their motive is."

I looked at them. "Did you see me get deactivated?"

Lee's eyes flicked up. "Yes."

He hesitated, as if choosing which part of the truth to hand me first.

"You shut down and hit the floor," he said. "You were out for at least three hours. Then you started glowing."

Raza's hands paused over the box, just long enough to show she was listening.

"I've never seen it," Lee continued. "Green lightning surrounded you. It lifted you off the deck like you weighed nothing, and then it rushed into your chest."

I felt my armor tighten, though nothing moved.

Lee swallowed. "You dropped again. Then *red* lightning exploded out of you. It wasn't a flicker. It was a burst. It lifted you almost to the ceiling."

My mind flashed to Alma's voice. Red. It suits you.

Lee went on, quieter now. "Voss came running in. He was in shock. His troops followed, but he sent them away. He stood over you like a man watching a miracle he didn't understand."

"Someone on his radio told him to kill you," Lee said. "Twice."

Raza's eyes narrowed, but she kept working, fingers adjusting the box's settings.

Lee's voice dropped further. "He didn't answer. He just watched."

"Then his radio crackled again," Lee said. "Kill him now, before it's too late."

I felt a slow chill crawl through my mind, the kind of cold that does not touch skin.

"And then?" I asked, though I already knew.

Lee looked at me. "That's when you woke up. Voss raised his weapon."

His gaze slid to Hensley's back at the controls, then returned to mine.

"And that's when the captain put him down."

"I was under the impression Voss brought me back just to kill me," I said.

"No," Lee replied. "You were already pulling yourself back."

Hensley cut in, voice tight. "Right now we have one option. We go to Ashen Gate."

Raza, Lee, and Michael snapped their heads toward him.

All the color drained from their faces.

Chapter Fifteen
Ashen Gate

In the distance, a single bright point flared into existence.

At first it looked like a star. Then a moon. Then it swelled, blooming outward like smoke in still air, the light thickening until it became a pale blue, luminous bruise against the dark.

The shape held, and the void around it seemed to bend, as if space itself was giving way.

Ashen Gate.

Hensley's voice had gone quiet when he first spoke the name, like a man naming something sacred and cursed at once.

A refuge for Humans of Flesh.

Not a paradise. Not safety. A place you ran to when every other door had closed.

After ash, we rebuild.

And this was the gate to the beginning.

But as it grew larger in the window, bright enough to sting even through the glass, one thought slid cold through my mind.

Why did Raza say they weren't welcome here?

I waited until the others were busy before I asked.

Raza stood near the viewport, arms folded, staring at nothing. She had the look of a woman rehearsing words she hoped she would never have to say.

"Ashen Gate," I said. "Why does everyone look like they're walking to the gallows?"

She didn't answer at first.

Then she exhaled, long and tired.

"Because we're not welcome," she said quietly.

I frowned. "It's a refuge."

"It was," she replied. "For people who followed the law."

She turned to face me.

"We stole the ship, Gregory."

The words landed dull at first, like they hadn't found their mark.

"You what?"

"We took it from Ashen Gate," she said. "Quietly. Carefully. We thought we were doing the right thing."

My thoughts started to sharpen.

"And the brains?"

Raza's jaw tightened.

"We took them too."

Silence filled the space between us, thick and suffocating.

"You took the brains?," I asked.

"We did," she said. "From Earth. From the research facility. From the Order."

She looked me in the eye.

"We had our own small army. The best pilots of the skies and space. All executed. The Order is powerful and ruthless."

The pieces began to slide into place.

"You didn't take them to use them," I said slowly.

"No," she replied. "We took them to save them."

She gestured toward the dark beyond the glass.

"To bring them somewhere the Order couldn't reach. Somewhere they could be put back into flesh. Somewhere human."

"Ashen Gate," I said.

"Yes."

"And they don't forgive theft," I said.

"They don't forgive disobedience," she corrected. "Especially when it puts their location and safety at risk."

I thought of Alma's calm smile.

Of how easily she let us go.

Of how the path had opened just a little too cleanly.

"They're going to follow us," I said.

Raza didn't deny it.

"We need Ashen Gate."

I stared back out at the light, no longer a distant glow but a looming horizon, close enough to feel we were falling into it.

Then the ice broke.

"But hey, you look worried for a robot." Raza nudged me with an elbow and a smile.

"This is the face they buried me with," I said with a smirk. "I guess they decided it was what I looked like."

Ashen Gate no longer looked like a refuge.

It looked like our last hope.

And I had a sinking feeling that this time, there would be no room for error.

The planet was almost entirely blue, a world of water that swallowed the light and then shone it back in deep, vibrant color. Only a few lumps of land broke the surface, rising from the ocean like scattered islands, dark green and lush.

They did not look worked. No roads cut through them. No gridlines. No smoke, no towers, no scars. Just forest, thick and untouched, treetops packed tight as fur and rolling over the hills in living silence.

From up here, it looked like a world that had never been claimed.

"Everyone in your seats. Belts on," Hensley announced.

The last motions in the pod turned frantic and small. Fingers flew over controls. Cabinets snapped shut. Latches clicked. Loose equipment was shoved into place. Then, one by one, the crew hurried to our seats and strapped in.

Silence settled over the craft, heavy and waiting.

Through the forward windows, the planet filled the glass. Blue everywhere, broken only by dark green islands and thick forests. We were minutes from the upper air. Close enough that the pod's hull began to gently shake in a new pitch, as if the atmosphere ahead was a cobble road.

Then something moved in the darkness around us.

Six small satellites slid into view, silent and precise. They spread out and began to orbit the pod in a tight ring, circling faster with each pass.

Thin beams of blue light snapped on.

They crawled over the hull in lines, then in grids, then in tight spirals, as if the satellites were reading every inch of us. The light passed over the windows and I felt it in my head, a cold pressure, like fingers testing the inside of my skull. The beams pulsed, paused, then pulsed again.

Scanning.

Cataloging.

Marking us for the record.

A voice cracked through the radio, flat and cold.

"Escape pod from Pilgrim's Wake. State your name and souls aboard."

Hensley swallowed once. His hands tightened on the controls.

"Captain Hensley," he said. "Six souls."

Silence.

Not static. Not interference.

The kind of silence that meant our answers were being compared against something already known.

Then the pod stopped.

Not slowed. Stopped.

My body lurched forward so hard the belt bit into my chest. Around me, straps snapped tight, seats groaned, and someone gasped as the air left their lungs in a rush.

The stars outside did not move. The planet hung in the window like a painted wall.

Michael's hands flew over the controls.

"Nothing," he whispered. "I'm locked out."

The voice returned, calmer now, as if we had already been judged.

"We have assumed control of your craft. You will be escorted to the Ashen Council for questioning. You are under arrest."

Static.

"Any attempt to resist will be met with lethal force."

The pod moved forward without the sound of engines.

It was pulled, as if an unseen hand had hooked us by the spine and started reeling us in.

The planet swelled in the windows. Blue became everything.

Then the first bite of atmosphere caught the hull.

CRASH.

The pod jolted so hard my teeth clacked together. The straps dug into my chest and shoulders, holding me in place while the world tried to rip me forward.

Outside, fire bloomed along the glass, orange and violent, licking across the pod as we plunged deeper. The flames did not roar the way they should. There was no air out there to feed them. Still, the heat shimmered and the light poured over us like a furnace door thrown open.

The pod began to shake and rattle, metal screaming in small, tired complaints. Every bolt felt loose. Every panel felt thin. The pod was never built for comfort. It was built for one thing.

Escape.

And now it felt like a coffin being dropped from the sky.

The vibrations eased, one tremor at a time, until the pod stopped rattling like it might tear itself apart.

The view beyond the windows sharpened.

Pure beauty.

The ocean below caught the sun and scattered it back in a thousand pieces, glittering as if the surface were strewn with diamonds. Wide sheets of cloud drifted over the water in slow procession, white and enormous, sailing across the blue like ships that needed no wind.

Green land rose in distant lumps, crowned with forest so dense it looked painted on, untouched by smoke or blade.

For a moment I forgot the straps across my chest. Forgot the cold voice on the radio. Forgot the satellites and their blue net.

A sight like that made even captivity feel smaller, almost harmless.

Almost.

Because beauty like this did not mean mercy.

It only meant the cage was built somewhere lovely.

The water rushed up at us.

Our pod showed no sign of slowing. No flare. No lift. Just a steep, committed dive.

Details snapped into focus. The texture of the waves. Whitecaps tearing themselves apart. The surface flexing like muscle beneath skin.

The ocean rose to meet us like a slap.

I braced, eyes narrowing, waiting for impact.

At the last instant, the sea changed.

The water beneath us began to turn.

Slow at first. Then tighter. Faster. The surface pulled inward, collapsing into itself as the center dropped away, the ocean drilled hollow in a single, violent motion.

A whirlpool opened beneath us.

The funnel stretched downward, smooth and vertical, leading straight into the deep.

We did not pull up.

We plunged.

The world outside the windows twisted into a spiraling blur. Light vanished in layers. Blue bruised to black. Then nothing remained but darkness pressing against the glass.

And still we fell.

At last, the descent eased.

The blind drop softened into control, and faint light seeped back into view. At first only a glow, just enough to reveal walls of water rising straight up around us.

A corridor carved from the sea itself.

The light strengthened, the darkness peeling away until the water glowed a clear, luminous blue, like an aquarium built for giants.

Life exploded into view.

Fish flashed past in silver and green, swarming and scattering, their bodies catching the light like thrown coins. They surged alongside the pod, riding our wake, then vanished just as quickly.

Below us, the ocean floor took shape, vast and shadowed.

The pod slowed further, impossibly gentle now, until it settled into a quiet hover.

Ahead, the water began to spin again.

The wall of blue peeled open, revealing a vertical passage of air. The sea parted cleanly, exposing a massive stone form beneath it.

Not a structure.

A mountain.

We drifted forward.

The water around the stone churned into white foam, spinning so violently it hid the true shape of what lay beyond. Through the blur I caught only fragments, flashes of rock carved with deliberate precision. Vast. Alien.

The pod crawled closer.

The ocean shuddered.

Seams split the stone face. A massive slab rolled aside, grinding rock against rock, revealing a cavern large enough to swallow cities.

A hollowed mountain.

We slipped inside.

Landing gear deployed with a dull clunk. A heartbeat later, metal kissed stone. The pod exhaled.

Outside the windows, there was no more water. No light.

Only rock.

The satellites that had escorted us through the descent released and drifted away. In tight formation, they spiraled back through the opening and vanished into the water tunnel beyond.

Then the door began to close.

The stone slab rolled into place. Foam and light disappeared behind it. The last thread of blue vanished.

The seal slammed shut.

Silence.

But not for long.

A blood-curdling scream tore through the pod.

We all snapped toward the sound at once.

Calder.

He was upright on the stretcher, eyes blown wide, chest heaving as he stared at the dark stone beyond the hull like he expected fire to burst through it.

"It's hell!" he shouted, voice cracking. "I'm sorry. Please, God, forgive me!"

I was on him in a step, gripping his shoulders, shaking him hard enough to jolt him back into the moment.

"Calder," I said, fast and firm. "Calder, look at me. Breathe. You're not in hell."

His eyes locked onto mine, wild and glassy.

"It's a long story," I added, lowering my voice, forcing calm into it. "But you need to listen. Relax. Just go with it for now."

He swallowed, body still trembling.

"We're in trouble," I said.

That cut through.

His gaze flicked past me to the others, then back again, fear sharpening into something more focused.

"Who are these people?" he asked. "Are these the ones we were trying to save?"

"Yes," I said quietly. "Mission success."

"Fuck," Calder said.

I glanced at the sealed entrance, then back at him.

"And just so you know," I added, "we're about to be arrested."

He blinked, like his mind refused to process a second disaster so soon.

Raza and Lee were already at the diagnostic panel. Raza leaned over the display, breathing hard.

"His readings are stronger than ever," she said. "Whatever was telling his body to hibernate lost connection the moment the cave sealed."

Lee didn't look up.

"And there are miles of water above us."

Calder froze.

"Miles of… what?"

"Water," Lee said. "Ocean."

Calder stared at him. Then at the ceiling, as if expecting the sea to start leaking through.

"Oh. Perfect," he said. "So I'm not in hell. I'm just buried under an ocean."

He threw his hands up toward the stone.

"This is what I get for trying to do the right thing."

He squinted at the walls pressing in around us.

"The galaxy's most aggressive inconvenience."

Raza snorted before she could stop herself.

Calder rubbed his temples, yanking the wires free from his head.

"No good deed goes unpunished."

He looked at me, humor fading just enough to let something sharper through.

"Next time," he said, mouth twisting into a smirk, "put me down as DNR."

"Welcome back, Calder," Hensley said, forcing a thin smile.

Then the smile vanished.

"But we need to get serious," he continued. "There are troops marching toward us. Right now."

We crowded the windows.

Outside, ranks of soldiers advanced across the stone floor in perfect formation, weapons raised. Not a battle. An arrest.

Behind us, the bottom hatch of the pod released with a hiss. The ramp unfolded and extended to the ground like a tongue.

A voice boomed from the formation, amplified until it filled the chamber and rattled in my skull.

"Drop all weapons and exit the pod with your hands raised. Any resistance will be met with lethal force."

No negotiation. No room to breathe.

Hensley swallowed once, and stood up straighter.

"Single file," he said quietly. "Do exactly as they say."

He went first. Then me. Calder. Michael. Raza. Lee.

We stepped down the ramp into the open, the stone was cold beneath our feet, the air heavy with salt and metal. You can feel the weight of the ocean above our heads.

"Line up," barked a field officer. "Side by side. On your knees. Hands on your heads."

We obeyed.

Kneeling there felt worse than a fight. This was chess. Every second stretched, daring me to make the first mistake.

Six soldiers approached, slow and cautious, each one keeping a weapon trained on a specific head. Their boots struck the floor in step, like a drumbeat calling an execution.

A guard in a black uniform marked POLICE came up behind us. He snapped metal cuffs onto Hensley's crew with quick, efficient clicks.

When he reached Calder and me, he did not use metal.

Blue lightning snapped into place around our wrists, tightening like constricting snakes.

Then another figure approached.

He did not hurry. He did not posture. He walked straight to Hensley as if the rest of us were furniture.

He stopped in front of Hensley.

"I'm disappointed in you."

The words were quiet. Worse for it.

"You committed treason," he said. "Grand theft. Murder."

Rifles remained leveled. No one shifted. The chamber held its breath.

"And then," he continued, eyes narrowing, "you did the one thing I warned would end us."

He turned and pointed.

Not at Hensley.

At me.

Then Calder.

"The moment you brought them back," he said, voice sharpening, "you turned this refuge into a coordinate."

He let the accusation hang.

"You didn't just betray Ashen Gate," he said. "You endangered it."

Hensley shook his head. "You don't understand. They can help us destroy the Order."

A humorless sound escaped the man's throat.

"The only thing you destroyed was our own military," he said. "You lost our ship. You lost our people. And you brought the enemy to our door."

He looked at us again.

"These bodies are not vessels," he said coldly. "They are beacons."

Hensley went pale.

"You think the Order lets its property walk away?" the man continued. "You think they let their soldiers desert?"

He spread his hands.

"You didn't bring salvation," he said. "You brought the hunt."

"Pardon me," Lee said, forcing the words out. "My readings show they were beacons. Not anymore."

A few heads turned.

"Under this much water, this much stone, Calder's suit has no external connection," Lee said quickly. "The signal can't escape."

The general's jaw flexed.

"And Gregory's suit," Lee added, pointing at me before he lost his nerve, "isn't receiving orders at all. It's operating independently."

Lee's face reflected the anomaly he witnessed.

"I saw the change," Lee said. "The energy interaction. The behavior shift. It's not standard anymore."

He hesitated.

"Jailbroken."

The word hardened the room.

"Enough," the general snapped.

Lee went silent.

"You don't understand what you've done," the general said, stepping forward. The soldiers behind him adjusted without being told. "Ashen Gate survives because it is unfound. A rumor. A dead coordinate."

His gaze cut from Hensley to me to Calder.

"One trace," he said. "One careless pulse."

His hand closed into a fist.

"That's all the Order needs."

He looked straight at Hensley.

"And you gave it to them."

Chapter Sixteen
PRISON

In captivity yet again. Isolation.

They separated us and put each of us in our own cell. Everything was white. No bars. No window.

There was nothing. Not even a bed. No toilet. Though the room was bright, it might as well have been pitch black.

I stood like a statue, but my mind was running. Alone with my thoughts is a severe punishment. If hell is not a physical place, and a man is only a soul when all else is taken, then this is truly what hell is.

Thoughts.

Hiss and clank. The door opened.

Two guards entered in step. One peeled to the right corner, the other to the left, rifles leveled on me the entire time. Then the general walked in behind them.

"Someone bring two chairs," he ordered.

He stood in the center of the white room, silent, studying me as if he could measure the shape of my thoughts.

Two more guards appeared at once, each carrying a chair. They set them facing each other, six feet apart, then withdrew without a word. His men moved like extensions of his own will, as if the command had traveled through a single spine.

"Please," Ashcroft said. "Have a seat, Gregory."

He gestured to the chair nearest me.

"My name is General Ashcroft. I have questions."

He sat opposite me, posture unmoving, hands resting on his knees like he was carved that way.

"First," he said, "what is your rank?"

"It depends who you ask," I said.

Ashcroft's eyes tightened. Irritated. Almost offended by the idea that an answer could refuse to be simple.

"Excuse me?" he said. "I am asking you."

"I was a private," I said. "Continental Army. Infantry."

The words landed flat. Honest. Unimpressive by design.

Ashcroft's brow twitched, just slightly. Not surprise. Confirmation.

"A private," he repeated. "No command. No authority. No voice."

"I carried a musket," I said. "I marched when told. I fired when ordered. I froze. I starved. And I watched men die beside me. I even watched myself die."

He studied me again, longer now, as if reassessing the weight of something he had already dismissed.

"So you were not chosen to lead," he said. "You were chosen to endure."

I met his gaze.

"I wasn't chosen at all," I said. "I was used."

The silence that followed was sharper than accusation.

Ashcroft leaned back in his chair, fingers steepled.

"And now," he said slowly, "what is it that you want?"

"Justice."

For the first time, something small moved behind his eyes. Interest. Not sympathy. Not approval. Just attention.

"Your friend, Calder." His voice stayed even. "Do you trust him?"

"With my life."

"Good." He nodded once. "Then we start on him right away."

A cold knot tightened in my mind. "Start what?"

"That body of his will be useless beyond these gates," he said. "So we are giving him a new one."

He let that sit, watching the impact.

"I have a plan for you two," he added.

"Whatever you're planning," I said, "I need my whole team."

Ashcroft's mouth curved, barely. "What team?"

"Calder," I said. "Hensley. Raza. Lee. Michael. And me."

I held his gaze.

"We leave together."

"You have some nerve for a private," he said. "That is my decision to make. But at this point, it's in God's hands."

The name hit me harder than any threat.

God.

I stared at him, certain I had misheard.

"You speak of God," I said carefully, "as if He is not forbidden here."

Ashcroft's expression did not change, but his eyes sharpened, as if he had finally found the part of me that mattered.

"Forbidden," he repeated, almost tasting the word. "To the Order, perhaps."

I shook my head once.

"In their world, death is a problem to be solved. The body is a cancer. And the soul is just a brain's activity."

"And that is why they are hollow," Ashcroft said.

He leaned forward, voice steady.

"You thought God was forgotten," he said. "You thought time buried Him."

I didn't answer, because it was true.

Ashcroft's gaze held mine.

"Listen to me, Gregory. Flesh remembers what metal tries to erase." He tapped two fingers lightly against his own chest. "Human of Flesh do not need permission to believe. We carry God the way we carry pain. The way we carry love. It is part of us, whether we speak it aloud or not."

The room went quiet around his words.

"So yes," he said, calmer now, "it is in God's hands."

He paused.

"And if you are truly a man of the past, then you already know what that means."

His eyes narrowed slightly, not unkind.

"It means you do your part. And you pray He does the rest."

Chapter Seventeen

Flight

"Let's take a walk," Ashcroft suggested.

I rose at once, before he could reconsider. The chair scraped softly against the white floor.

"Lead on," I said. "I have stared at blank walls long enough."

A faint shift crossed his face, something between amusement and appraisal.

"You want to see Ashen Gate," he said.

"Who wouldn't, after an entrance like that?"

Ashcroft held my gaze, then turned toward the door. The guards in the corners pointed their guns down like I was no longer a threat.

"Keep pace," he said, and the door hissed open.

We walked the corridor in silence. Cells lined both sides, countless as piano keys. From inside they appeared as smooth white slabs, seamless and blind, and the outside, brutal stone.

And as we passed, faint windows revealed themselves only at certain angles, narrow panes cut into the rock and hidden by the light. A combination of nature and science.

Everything here was stone. Not veneer. Not assembled. Carved. The walls bore the subtle scars of tools, as if the ocean rock itself had been hollowed out and shaped into order. The air felt dense, cool, and still, carrying a salt-metal tang that clung to the back of my throat.

My thoughts kept circling the same fact like a vulture.

We were deep beneath the sea.

Not a ship above water. Not a cave near shore. Buried under miles of black weight, held down by an ocean that could crush a man without ever touching him.

Something about it unsettled me more than the stars ever had. In space, at least, there was emptiness. You could imagine escape. You could imagine distance.

Here, the world pressed in from every direction. Above us was not sky, but water, and the knowledge of it sat on my mind like a stone.

I glanced at Ashcroft. He walked as if the depth meant nothing.

We approached a large door, which opened as Ashcroft placed his hand on a screen. We left the prison room and made our way to a dark platform that faced a tube with an oval opening.

We stood in silence.

A sound gaining volume cried with speed and pitch. Something was moving toward us in the tube. The noise was deafening echoing off the surrounding stone.

A hiss and a clunk.

In the opening appeared a capsule with eight seats. Ashcroft jumped in first and patted the seat next to him. I sat down and the door slid shut.

Ashcroft pressed a button.

Without warning, the transport capsule shot off with incredible speed. Pinning me down to the seat. We shot like a musket ball. Up, down, left right. A blur of light was all I could see through the window.

The capsule began to slow with a deep whining sound and then we were still. I got out stumbling. It took a moment for my senses to adjust. Then the space unfolded before me.

The chamber was carved from stone, but it did not feel enclosed. The ceiling rose so high it blurred into shadow, and the walls bent away until they seemed to dissolve into the distance. It felt less like standing inside a structure and more like standing beneath a sky that had been buried.

A hollowed out mountain.

And there were clouds.

Not painted, not imagined. Real masses of pale vapor drifting slow across the upper dark, gathering and thinning as if the air itself had weather. They moved lazily, silent and indifferent, like they belonged to a world above ground.

The scale swallowed sound. Swallowed thought.

Larger than a city square. Larger than anything I've ever seen built by hands.

"What is this place?" I asked in awe.

"Today, you're learning to fly." He pointed at familiar looking crafts. These were the same iron birds that I saw when I first came to this world.

Ashcroft led me down a long bay carved into the stone, where a row of small craft sat waiting in perfect order. They were lined up wing to wing, neat as cavalry in a stable, quiet and patient.

I stared at them and felt my thoughts tighten.

I am going to get myself killed.

Ashcroft stopped beside one craft and rested a hand on its hull as if introducing me to a prized animal.

"You'll be flying this one," he said.

I stepped closer.

Even after everything I had seen, the thing was beautiful. Sleek. Clean. It was no doubt a creation of a human hand.

Its surface caught the light and threw it back in soft gray waves, as if it swallowed brightness and returned it richer. The cockpit glass curved like a clear shield, flanked by two wings sharp as blades. Beneath each wing sat two heavy guns, and another was mounted under the nose. Whatever else it was, this was a killing machine.

Inside were two seats, one behind the other. The cockpit looked oddly cozy. This was not engineered for utility alone. It was made for humans, by humans. The seats looked lined with fur, the yoke wrapped in leather, the controls arranged with a kind of familiar care, like someone expected a living hand to tremble on them.

For a heartbeat, I let myself take it in.

Then the moment broke.

A commotion rose behind us, sharp voices and the scrape of boots, coming from the direction of the transport capsule, the tube we had arrived through. The fuss grew louder, messy, human.

"What is this place? Get off me. This is ridiculous," someone shouted, fighting as he was hauled along.

I turned.

Calder was being escorted by two soldiers. He walked stiffly like a man learning his own legs again, and his voice carried the raw edge of panic that had nowhere to land. He looked different, though. Not flesh. Not the familiar green-lit armor.

A new body.

Built in the same general shape as before, only cleaner, stronger. But something looked different. Beneath his plating, a red light pulsed, slow and steady.

Calder's head snapped toward me when he saw us, and his outrage doubled.

Ashcroft watched him approach without the slightest concern.

"Gregory," Ashcroft said, calm as ever, "meet your new co-pilot."

Calder stopped short as if the words had struck him.

"What?" he barked. "Co-pilot?"

He looked from Ashcroft to me, then back again, incredulous.

"First I end up under your command," he said, pointing at me, "and you have never led a day in your life. Now you're the pilot, and you have definitely never flown before."

I held his gaze and kept my voice even, as if I still had a body that could steady it.

"It's called composure," I said, half joking, half warning. "If you manage to keep yours, maybe you'll rise."

Calder stared at me like he wanted to argue.

Then his eyes dropped, catching the red glow in his own chest.

Whatever he saw there stole the rest of his words.

His gaze drifted down to his chest, to the slow, pulsing red light beneath the plating. He lifted a hand, turned it once, flexed his fingers like he was testing a borrowed limb. The anger drained from his face, replaced by something quieter. Disbelief. Awe. Maybe grief.

He exhaled a long exaggerated breath and shook his head.

"Did they really have to make us look so… matchy-matchy?" he said at last, forcing a crooked grin. "I mean, if we're going to die, I was hoping to at least keep my own style."

The joke landed thin, stretched tight over something fragile.

He glanced back up at me, eyes searching, as if making sure I was still there, still real.

"I don't know how I feel about this yet," he added more softly. "Feels like I woke up in someone else's skin."

"Welcome to the club," I said with a scoff.

Then he straightened, squared his shoulders, and gestured toward the lined-up craft with his chin.

"So," he said, voice steadier now, "which one of these beautiful mistakes are we about to crash?"

The cockpit canopy swung open with a soft hiss.

"I'm guessing it's that one." Calder started up the ladder and swung himself toward the rear seat.

"Calder," Ashcroft said, flat and final, "your seat is the one in front."

Calder froze halfway in, then looked back over his shoulder. "You're serious."

He climbed back down one rung at a time, slow, offended, and performing every second of it.

"So when we crash," he muttered, "I hit first."

He dropped to the deck, threw Ashcroft a look, slid the ladder over and climbed in. "Thanks."

I then climbed the ladder and dropped into my seat, hands finding the yoke. My only experience was watching Hensley launch an escape pod.

Below us, Ashcroft shouted, "Put on the headphones!"

"The what?" I yelled back.

"The headphones," he repeated, circling his own ears with both hands like a frantic ape.

"Ah. These." I watched Calder fit his on, then grabbed mine.

I stretched them over my head and leaned back.

The world muted. The cavern's vastness vanished, and the world felt small.

I stared at the panel of lights and switches and whispered to myself, "We are definitely done for."

"We are what?" Calder's voice snapped into my ears, clear as a bell.

I froze. "You can hear me?"

"Yes," he said. "Now get me out of here!"

Before I could answer, another voice cut in, calm and precise.

"Welcome to your flight training. I will guide you through your first launch, step by step. This craft is designated: Ashen Piercer."

The canopy began to close.

Glass swung down in a smooth arc and sealed with a soft, final hiss.

Now it felt real.

"Press the blinking red button to the right of the yoke," the voice instructed.

I found it and pressed.

The Piercer answered with a single deep roar, more felt than heard, and then settled into a permanent rumble that vibrated up my arms and into my teeth. The lights across the panel brightened in a clean sweep, like a dawn switching on.

Calder let out a low whistle in my ear. "That sounds expensive."

"Eyes forward," the voice said, not sharp, but final. "You are waking the core. Do not touch any other controls unless I tell you."

A thin line of blue light traced around the rim of the canopy, sealing tighter. My seat tightened around my ribs as if the craft wanted to make sure I stayed inside it.

"Step one," the voice continued. "Confirm your restraints are locked."

I looked down. The harness had cinched itself. I could not have loosened it if I tried.

"Locked," I said.

"Good. Step two. Place both hands on the yoke and hold steady. You are not steering yet. You are authorizing."

My fingers wrapped the rectangular grips. The yoke felt warm, almost alive, and for a moment the craft seemed to listen to my pulse, matching it.

"Step three," the voice said. "Thumb switch, left side of the yoke. Toggle to ARM."

I found the switch with my thumb and flipped it.

A soft chime sounded. The rumble deepened. Outside the canopy, faint lines of light crawled along the Piercer's wings and down into its belly, like veins filling.

"Hover system engaged," the voice said. "You will feel lift before you see movement. Do not fight it."

The floor beneath us stopped feeling like a floor. The Piercer lightened, as if the world had loosened its grip. The craft rose an inch, then another, no wheels, no scrape, just a quiet separation from the stone.

Calder's voice came tight in my ear. "We're floating."

"Step four," the voice said. "Nose thrusters. Dial to ONE."

A small wheel sat near my right knee, marked in thin ticks. I turned it to the first notch.

The Piercer rotated smoothly on its own axis, pivoting away from the line of parked craft. It moved like it had rehearsed this in my sleep, easing outward from wingtip to wingtip without touching anyone.

The lined-up Piercers beside us remained still, perfect as statues. Ours slid past them like a blade between ribs.

"Maintain hover," the voice said. "Do not overcorrect. Small inputs. This craft will amplify panic."

"I'm not panicking," I muttered.

Calder snorted. "That makes one of us."

"Step five," the voice continued. "Forward drift. Tap the top paddle on the yoke. Once."

I hesitated, then tapped.

The Piercer glided forward. Not fast. Not yet. A controlled, steady drift out into the open cavern, leaving the row behind us.

The rumble smoothed into something steadier, more confident, like it approved.

Below, tiny figures moved between the craft, looking up. Far ahead, the chamber opened wider, empty air waiting.

"Good," the voice said. "You are clear of the line."

The Piercer hovered there, poised, suspended over nothing but distance.

"Next," the voice said, "we will now introduce gentle flight."

I held the Piercer steady, hands firm on the yoke, muscles tight where muscles no longer truly mattered.

"Maintain your current attitude," the voice continued. "Do not push forward. Do not climb."

The craft hovered in place, engines humming evenly, suspended over nothing.

"Now," the voice said, "advance the throttle slightly."

I shifted my right hand back to the lever and eased it forward, no more than the width of a finger.

The response was immediate.

The Piercer did not lurch. It did not surge. It glided.

The vast chamber began to slide past us, stone walls drifting by as if the world itself were moving and we were standing still. The craft maintained its height, its balance, its calm.

"Good," the voice said. "That is forward flight."

I swallowed.

The sense of motion was strange. There was no wind, no vibration to announce speed. Only the quiet certainty that we were moving through an impossible space.

"Throttle controls speed only," the voice reminded me. "Direction remains with the yoke. Keep your inputs minimal."

I nudged the yoke a fraction to the left.

The Piercer rolled into a clean banking correction. I brought the yoke back a touch. The nose came up, the deck angle changing by degrees, and gravity pinned me a little harder into the seat as we started to climb.

Calder leaned forward in his seat.

"We're flying," he said, half laughing, half stunned. "We're actually flying."

I didn't answer.

The chamber opened wider ahead of us, clouds drifting far below, the floor falling away until it felt like we were crossing the sky itself.

"Maintain this pace," the voice said. "This is gentle flight. Learn it. Trust it."

I steadied my breathing.

For the first time since leaving my body, since waking beneath the soil, since being buried by centuries and machines, I felt something dangerously close to control.

The chamber continued to drift past us, stone and cloud sliding by in a slow, unreal calm.

For a moment, I almost believed I understood it.

Almost.

My hand tightened on the yoke, an old reflex rising before thought could stop it. Back home, when a horse hesitated, you did not ask. You told. A sharp pull. A snap of the reins.

I jerked the yoke back like reins on a horse.

The cabin snapped vertical.

My right hand slipped.

The throttle slammed forward.

The Piercer screamed upward.

Not climbed.

Not lifted.

It whipped.

The engines detonated into a furious howl and the craft shot straight up, crushing us into our seats as the ceiling rushed toward us. My vision blurred. My chest felt pinned. Calder shouted something incoherent through the headset.

"Incorrect input," the voice snapped, suddenly stripped of patience.

I panicked and reacted on instinct again, shoving the yoke forward.

The Piercer answered with equal violence.

We plunged.

The clouds surged up like a living wall. My stomach dropped away entirely as the craft snapped downward, engines shrieking in protest. The floor raced toward us.

I pulled up on the yoke.

"Gregory!" Calder yelled. "I swear to God"

I yanked the throttle back hard.

A sharp tone erupted in my headset.

"Warning. Stall. Warning. Stall."

The Piercer ceased to fly.

It dropped.

Not gently. Like an autumn leaf. Like the sky had simply let go of it.

My stomach should have fallen into my boots, but my body gave me nothing. Only a clear, brutal fact.

We were falling.

Spinning.

The nose pitched, the craft yawing as if it wanted to roll into a death spiral. The canopy filled with nothing but rushing dark stone and the suggestion of distance.

Instinct took the wheel.

Not thought. Not training. Instinct.

I shoved the yoke forward just enough to break the stall, forcing the nose down to bite air again. At the same time my feet found the pedals and I stamped hard, fighting the sideways slip, kicking the tail back in line before the fall could twist into a spin.

The warning screamed again.

"Warning. Stall. Warning. Stall."

I rammed the throttle forward.

The engines answered with a feral surge. The Piercer shuddered, caught, then jerked as the lift returned in a violent breath. The drop slowed. The yaw steadied. The craft stopped trying to kill us and became a machine again.

The Piercer leveled out hard, flying again, the engines strained and then settled back into their steady, ominous rumble.

Silence.

Calder's voice came through my headset, thin and breathless.

"This is BULLSHIT!"

I did not answer. My hands were locked on the controls like prayer.

Only then did the instructor speak.

"You recovered without instruction."

I did not like the way it said that.

Calder exhaled, a sound halfway between laughter and shock.

"So," he said, "no whipping the sky like a mule."

Just to silence him.

"Noted."

My hand returned to the throttle, slow this time. Deliberate.

Human habits die hard.

Machines are unforgiving.

Chapter Eighteen

PHANTOM

Pain came without warning.

It seized me whole, as if I were lifted by the skull and held over flame. There was no heat, no smoke, no flesh to burn, and yet my entire being screamed as though it remembered exactly how fire felt.

The pain did not belong to any one place. It had no center. It poured through me all at once, not sharp but absolute, a total occupation of thought. It was memory without context, sensation without source.

My body had no nerves left to betray me, but the mind carried its own map of suffering. Every place I once had skin, muscle, breath, it lit up in protest, phantom signals echoing from a life long gone.

I tried to brace, to recoil, to pull away, but there was nowhere to move. No muscles to tense. No teeth to grit. The pain was not something I endured. It was something I was.

And beneath it all was the most terrifying realization of all.

This was not damage nor a wound.

This was memory insisting on being felt.

This memory would come in waves. Crash without warning, sweep the sand on the beach, and recede back into the sea.

Now, slowly, pain's grip began to loosen.

Not like relief. Not like healing.

It dissolved the way smoke thins in still air, uneven and uncertain. One sensation faded while another lingered, flaring again as if offended at being dismissed. I did not put the fire out. It extinguished itself.

The screaming quieted into an ache, the ache into a pressure, the pressure into a distant footprint in the sand. What remained was not comfort, but absence. A hollow where agony had been, still warm, still watching.

I was left suspended in the aftermath, uncertain if the pain had ended or simply retreated, waiting for permission to return. Am I in the eye of the storm, or the end?

And in that quiet, I understood something worse than suffering.

The pain had not been in vain.

It had been my body remembering itself.

A body left behind as a sacrifice to the Order of the Earth.

Where I come from, sacrifice was something a man chose.

You laid your life down because you believed in something higher than yourself. You did not drag others onto the altar and call it destiny.

The Order calls what they do sacrifice, but it is theft. They take lives and strip them of flesh, of memory, of choice, then claim it was for the greater good.

God never demanded that kind of offering.

Only Satan.

Kings force their people to fight for causes that profit only kings. I have seen it before. Men sent into cold, into hunger, into death, not for freedom, but for titles they would never wear and lands they would never touch.

The Order is no different. If it prospers, what does the common man gain? A stronger chain. A quieter voice. A future where his body is no longer his own.

But if Ashen Gate prospers, man keeps what was always meant to be his. His flesh. His will. His faith. His freedom to stand or fall as himself.

So I will stand with Ashen Gate.

And if the Order wants my body again, they will have to take it from me.

Chapter Nineteen

THE VILLAGE

I walked the long stone corridor toward the underground village, the passage widening and narrowing in slow breaths. Ashen Gate was not a single chamber. It was a web, a living network of tunnels cut through the bedrock deep beneath the ocean floor. Some tunnels were for foot traffic and some were tubes for transport capsules. Every so often a side passage opened like a vein giving an alternative route, or a place to sit.

Tonight, I walked to reflect.

Not because I needed to. Not because anyone ordered me to. But because I wanted to. Lately, when I was alone with my thoughts, it never felt like my choice. Solitude kept finding me, locking me in white rooms, sealing me in gel, forcing me to listen to myself until reality turned obscure.

This time, I chose to mingle with my mind.

My steps clicked against stone, the rhythm steady and slow. The walls were smooth in places, as if polished by time, and rough in others, where the rock still looked freshly carved. Pale light seeped from thin seams in the ceiling, not bright enough to blind, not dim enough to hide. It made everything look clean, almost sacred, like a place built for quiet decisions.

I did not feel fatigue. I did not yawn. I did not carry that heavy sweetness behind the eyes that used to tell me night had come.

But I missed sleep.

Not the need for it, but the ritual. The simple mercy of closing my eyes and waking to a new day. Back then, no matter how brutal the march, no matter how cold the night, a man could surrender to darkness and let time carry him somewhere else for a while.

Now life did not reset.

It ran.

One continuous stretch of awareness. A single unbroken thread with no sleep, no night. Just thought after thought after thought, stacking like stones until even memory felt heavy.

Somewhere ahead, the corridor opened. I could feel it before I saw it, the air changing, the space widening. Faint sounds began to bleed in. Voices. Footsteps. The distant glide of a capsule passing through a tunnel like a whispering bullet.

A village, waiting at the end of stone.

And me, walking toward it, trying to remember what it felt like to be human.

The village stretched far beneath me.

The tunnel I arrived through was elevated, carved high into the stone like a ledge. It felt like standing on a cliff, looking down on a world that should not exist under miles of ocean. The ceiling arched overhead in a vast dome, its curve disappearing into shadow.

Below, Ashen Gate lived.

Clusters of homes were built into terraces and ridges, their walls smooth and pale, their roofs rounded and practical. Narrow lanes threaded between them, busy with movement. There were markets with canvas-like awnings and stalls arranged in neat rows. Voices carried up in soft layers, not loud, just constant, like the city was always speaking to itself.

And there were farms.

Small patches of green, carefully contained, bright against the stone. Rows of low crops grew in raised beds. Vines climbed trellises that had been anchored into the rock. Water ran in thin channels cut with precision, glinting as it moved, feeding life in controlled streams. It was not wilderness. It was man-made. But the human touch made it feel like home.

At the center of it all stood two towers.

They rose taller than the surrounding structures, clean pillars of carved stone and engineered metal, like twin spines holding the village upright. Their purpose was obvious even from here, not in the way they looked, but in the way the whole city seemed to keep time with them.

On the first tower, a massive light sat on a swivel, slow and deliberate, rotating with the day. It cast a warm glow that climbed the curve of the dome and spilled across it, then poured back down over rooftops, farms, and market lanes. As it moved, the light shifted in tone and intensity, emulating a sun's long arc. Morning. Noon. Late afternoon. Dusk.

The second tower waited.

When the first dimmed, the other woke. Its light was cooler, thinner, and steadier. A pale circle that glided across the dome like a moon among a constellation of stars, casting soft shadows and quiet silver over the village below.

Together, they made time feel real.

Tonight, the moon was full.

Its pale light washed across the village, soft but generous, helping everything below glow. Stone paths shimmered faintly. Roofs shined and sparkled. Even the leaves in the small terrace farms seemed to drink it in.

Below me, life moved on.

People hustled and bustled through the streets, carrying baskets, closing stalls, laughing, arguing, living as if they were not hidden beneath an ocean and hunted by forces far greater than themselves. Children ran between adults. Lanterns were lit. Doors opened and shut. Meals were shared.

They walked with the quiet confidence of people who had already decided that fear would not rule them any longer. As if danger were a distant rumor, not a weight pressing down through miles of water and stone.

The village was inviting. An urge rose in me, sudden and almost painful, to descend those stairs and walk the cobbled streets, just to feel human again.

I started down the zigzagging steps carved into the village wall.

A familiar voice boomed behind me.

"Whoa, whoa, whoa," the voice echoed. "You're going to cause quite a stir looking like that. Let's get you a change of clothes."

Raza stood there with Michael and Lee, all three of them wearing the same look: half concern, half disbelief, but full of smiles.

I glanced down at myself and understood immediately.

Red lights pulsed beneath my armor. Plates still scuffed from the ship. Weapon marks. Blood stains I had stopped noticing.

In a quiet village trying to pretend it was still a village, what would I look like?

A war machine strolling into a marketplace like a sudden takeover was in play.

I couldn't help it. A laugh broke out of me, sharp and sudden.

"Ha," I said. "I'm so happy to see you guys."

Raza came down the last few steps in a rush and threw her arms around me. For a moment I froze, caught between caution and disbelief. Then my arms moved on their own and closed around her.

Even through steel, even through the cold borrowed body I wore, her warmth reached something in me that nothing else had. My mind, always sprinting, stalled for a single breath. The village below looked brighter. The war did not vanish, but it moved farther away, like thunder rolling off toward another valley.

One hug.

I should have let go sooner.

I did not want to.

But I eased my grip, careful, as if I might break the moment by holding it too tightly. She loosened too. Then we stepped apart.

"All right," I said, and my voice came out steadier than I felt. "Where do we go?"

Raza's eyes flicked over my armor, quick and practical, measuring what could be hidden and what could not.

"Somewhere private," she said. "Before a kid sees you and starts screaming, and then the whole village starts asking questions we can't answer."

She turned and moved off on a mission. Michael and Lee fell in beside her.

For the first time in a long time, I followed.

We moved through the corridors again, and this time they felt familiar. Raza and the others walked with ease, as if every turn belonged to them. The tunnel felt brighter with company. Lighter. Belonging has a way of changing a place.

"What became of Hensley?" I asked, careful not to fracture the moment.

Michael didn't answer right away.

"He's still locked up," he said at last.

Raza glanced back at me. "The Council separated us for questioning. You and Calder were pulled out first."

I frowned. "Why?"

"Because Hensley asked them to," Lee said.

I stopped walking.

"He stood up during his interrogation," Michael said, voice steady.

Raza added, "He told them Pilgrim's Wake leaving port was his decision alone."

My chest tightened.

"He told them that you and Calder rescued us," Michael said. "That you were heroes."

Lee swallowed. "He made it very clear that if someone had to answer for defying a direct order, it would be him."

Michael looked ahead as we walked. "He told them Ashen Gate needed engineers more than it needed another captain who thought he knew better than the Council."

"They wanted to detain all of us," Lee added. "We technically 'broke our engineering oath' for not reporting."

"Hensley cut that off fast," Michael said.

We walked in silence for a few steps.

"I can't believe it," I said. "He seemed too principled for something like this."

"Yes," Raza replied. "Part of the reason they didn't shame him. Anyone else would have been executed, given the number of soldiers we lost."

"Such a good man fighting for what he thought was right…what *was* right. He tried to *save* our people. I'm surprised they wouldn't understand." I said.

Raza met my eyes. "Because leadership carries consequence. And precedent."

Michael added, "If Ashen Gate forgives a captain for stealing a ship just because he believed in the cause, then tomorrow another captain does the same. And the next one might be wrong."

Lee's voice dropped. "Hensley said that himself."

I exhaled slowly.

"He asked them to hold him," Raza said. "Until the war is decided."

"And after?" I asked.

No one answered immediately.

Finally, Michael said, "After that, Ashen Gate will decide whether his choice saved us… or endangered everything."

We reached the end of the corridor. Warm light from another village spilled across the stone.

As we stepped into it, one truth settled heavy in my chest.

Hensley wasn't confined because Ashen Gate feared him.

He was confined because Ashen Gate believed responsibility mattered.

And because he chose to carry it alone.

"This way," Raza said, hopping down the steps.

We worked our way down the steep, carved staircase and slipped through the village's shadows. The cobbled paths below were quieter than the markets above, lit by the false moon and the occasional lantern glow from doorways.

Then, around a corner on an empty path, I saw a silhouette I could not mistake.

The figure moved slowly, shoulders drawn in, head bowed as if he were studying his own feet for answers. Lost in thought.

It was an unusual posture for him.

But, I've seen this look many times.

A soldier.

Calder.

For a moment, something in me tightened. Just the sense that he was fighting something with no shape.

But I let it go. We had all been dragged through too much. If I started trying to weigh every silence, I would never stop.

So I did what felt simpler.

I crept up behind him and threw my arms around him.

For half a heartbeat, he went rigid. Then we sprang apart like opposing magnets.

The embrace did not land the way it had with Raza.

Calder staggered back a step, staring at me like I had malfunctioned.

"What the hell was that?" he demanded, equal parts disgusted and stunned.

"A hug," I said, instantly regretting it.

Raza, Lee, and Michael burst into laughter.

Lee wiped at his eyes. "Come with us," he said. "You two are getting a makeover."

Passing lines of dwellings, we eventually reached a door set flush into the stone, so seamless it looked carved rather than built. Lee lifted his hand to the panel.

A soft tone chimed. Light swept over his palm.

The door slid open.

Lee stepped aside with theatrical pride. "Here we are."

Inside, the dwelling was spherical, neat, and minimal, like it had been carved by an artist. The curved walls were smooth and pale, the seams so tight they almost disappeared. Light bled softly from narrow strips set into the ceiling's radius, warm enough to feel welcoming without ever becoming bright.

To the left was a compact kitchen tucked into the curve. Everything was built into the wall: a counter that folded out cleanly, cabinets that sat flush until touched, and a round window above the sink that looked into the village like a porthole. A few simple cups rested in a perfect line, and a small basin held water that shimmered faintly.

Near the center sat a small table anchored to the floor, circular to match the room, with three stools that could slide beneath it. Nothing was wasted. Nothing was cluttered. Every object had a place.

I thought of my kids.

If they were here, there'd be crumbs on the floor, fingerprints on the window, and a cup missing for reasons no man could explain.

I took their little messes for granted.

Disorder and imperfections really make a place come to life.

Beyond the table, the living area opened up. A horseshoe-shaped couch hugged the curve of the far wall, fitted exactly to the radius, its cushions soft and worn in a way that suggested real bodies had actually lived here. A folded blanket lay draped over one arm, and a low shelf held a few small personal items, not many, but enough to prove the place belonged to someone and not just a system.

But the room was not as spotless as it pretended to be.

Off to the right, tucked into a recess of the curved wall, was another section entirely. A desk had been built into the stone like an afterthought, and it looked like a storm had hit it and never left.

Papers were scattered everywhere, some pinned under mugs, others sliding off the edge in curling stacks. Books lay open and face-down, spines cracked, pages marked with frantic notes. The surface was crowded with scribbled symbols and numbers, lines drawn and crossed out and rewritten, as if someone had been fighting the universe with math and refusing to lose.

Lee's kind of mess.

It was the first thing in the dwelling that felt truly alive. Not designed. Not curated. Worked in. Lived in.

Raza, Lee, and Michael dropped back into the couch and released a unified, heavy breath. They looked like people who had been holding themselves upright for days and had finally been permitted to stop.

Raza leaned forward, reached for a tablet on the low shelf, and brought it onto her lap. The screen woke with a dim glow. She began tapping, quick and practiced, eyes narrowing slightly as she worked.

I watched her hands without meaning to. The way they moved was calm, precise, and gentle. Not the harsh efficiency of machines. Something softer. Human. Her brow drew into a faint frown as she typed, a small crease of concentration that captured my gaze.

"So," Raza asked, flicking her eyes up at us and back to the screen as if pulling data from the air, "what's your style?"

Calder and I just stared at each other.

Blank.

The room held the silence for half a second, and then Lee snorted. Michael laughed first, then harder, and soon it became contagious.

Raza broke too, lifting her hand like she was surrendering. "Of course," she said, half laughing, half sighing. "Of course you two have no style."

Calder lifted his hands a little, palms out, as if presenting himself. "This is style," he said dryly.

Raza snorted, thumbs tapping. "No," she said. "That's not style, Calder. That's 'man who sleeps in his armor.'"

Calder and I traded a glance.

He didn't have to say it.

We don't sleep.

She went right back to the tablet, fingers flying, and said, "Perfect."

Then, without looking up, she added, "Gregory, you're first. Bedroom down the hall. Remove your armor, then step into the shower and press the green button on your left."

Two thoughts collided in my mind at once.

First: There's another room?

This place seemed to keep unfolding, space appearing where I didn't expect it, like the village itself was alive and rearranging around us.

Second: How exactly am I supposed to remove the armor?

I glanced down at myself, at the seamless plates, the locked joints, the quiet glow beneath it all. No clasps. No straps. Nothing that resembled a way out.

I started toward the hall anyway, because that's what I've learned to do when I don't understand something yet.

Behind me, I caught a flicker of anxious laughter. Not mocking. Anticipatory. Like they knew something I didn't.

I walked on, unsure whether I was about to discover a simple solution…

Or embarrass myself spectacularly.

The room sealed before I could change my mind.

A low vibration rose from the walls. From the floor. From inside me.

My armor activated without command.

Internal locks disengaged in sequence, the sensation crawling beneath my awareness, subtle at first, then unmistakable. It felt like movement under the surface. Like something waking.

I tried to lift my arm.

It did not answer.

The armor began to open on its own, plates separating with a sound that was far too deliberate. Not rushed. Not careful. Just automatic. As if this ritual had been performed countless times before I ever existed.

Cold air slipped in as the plating withdrew, and beneath it was not bone or wire.

It was skin.

Artificial. Seamless. Smooth.

A soft gold glow pulsed beneath it, slow and rhythmic, like a heartbeat trying to remember how to beat. But the light did not remain still. It shifted. Rippled.

Just beneath the surface, shapes moved.

Not fast. Not frantic.

Small disturbances traveled under the skin, like insects tunneling through soil. A faint rise here. A subtle slide there. As if something mechanical and alive was rearranging itself, settling into place.

I wanted to look away.

I couldn't.

The gold pulse illuminated the movement, turning it almost beautiful if I didn't think too hard about what it meant. Whatever lived beneath that skin was not meant to be seen. And yet here it was, exposed to air, to sight, to judgment.

I felt nothing where the armor released me. No pain. No relief.

Only the awareness that this body remembered sensations my mind no longer owned.

Piece by piece, the shell peeled back, each segment unlocking with quiet clicks. With every release, I felt less contained. Less defined. As if the armor had not been restraining me, but holding me together.

When the final seal disengaged, I swayed.

Nothing remained to brace me.

Behind me, the armor stood upright and still, hollow.

Then without warning, it folded down to the size of a Bible.

I stepped into the shower stall and found the button Raza had mentioned. A small green circle set into the wall, calm as an eye.

I pressed it.

A soft hiss answered. Warm vapor rolled in, thick and clean, swallowing the room until even the corners disappeared. Steam wrapped my body in a gentle pressure, clinging to the gold sheen of my skin and blurring it into something almost human.

I stood there, still as stone, while the air worked.

No scrubbing. No water. Just heat, scent, and something else, a faint electrical tingle that crawled across my surface like invisible fingertips. It was intimate in a way that made me uneasy. As if the house itself was measuring me. Learning me.

Then, as quickly as it came, the steam thinned.

The fog peeled away in ribbons and vanished, leaving the stall dry and silent.

I blinked and looked down.

Clothes.

A dark fitted top, smooth and clean, cut close to the body. Pants the same, tapered and sharp, with a faint sheen that caught the light and returned it in muted waves. The fabric looked soft.

There were boots too. Simple. Sleek. Black. No laces. No buckles. They looked like they would lock to my feet and never let go.

And then the strangest piece.

A small cap of knitted cloth, soft-looking, meant to hug the skull. No brim. No shape like a soldier's hat. Just a snug, dark crown you pulled down over your head, like a second skin.

On a small shelf, sat a pair of dark lenses framed in thin black material. Glass meant to cover the eyes.

To hide my glowing eyes.

I stared at them for a moment longer than I meant to.

So they knew.

They knew my eyes were wrong. They knew the gold under my skin could betray me. They knew a village full of children and merchants would stare, and staring would turn to fear, and fear would turn to questions.

Raza was not just dressing me.

She was disguising me.

The dark lenses. I slid them onto my face.

The world dimmed a shade, softer at once. Then my artificial eyes recalibrated, and the darkness behind the lenses thinned to brightness again.

For the first time since waking in this metal prison, I looked at my reflection in the glass and did not immediately feel like a machine.

Just a man.

Or close enough.

Somewhere outside the door, I heard laughter.

My hand hovered near the handle.

I took one breath I did not need, and still found myself taking it anyway. I have fought battles no regular man could stomach, but walking back to my new "friends" dressed like this filled me with a sharper kind of dread.

Then I opened the door and stepped back into the living room.

"Whoa!" The room went wild, cheers and applause bouncing off the curved walls like we had just won a battle.

I shook my head, smiling despite myself. "You people need hobbies."

Calder leaned forward on the couch, eyes sweeping me up and down like a tailor with an attitude. He gave an approving nod.

"Now you look good enough to hug me," he said, spreading his arms wide.

Raza laughed into her hand. Lee nearly choked. Michael's shoulders shook like he was trying not to join in.

Calder pointed at me. "No. You started this. You hugged me in the street."

"I did not," I said, though my grin betrayed me. "And you recoiled like I was on fire."

"I am not built for affection," Calder declared. "I am built for war and mild sarcasm."

"Quiet," I said, stepping aside and motioning toward the hall. "You're next."

Calder's confidence evaporated instantly. His hands went to his chest like I had just sentenced him. "Next… as in… I have to do the steam thing?"

"Yes."

He stared at the doorway like it led to an execution.

He nodded once, resigned. "Right. Armor off. Dignity next." Then, quieter, "Just make sure nobody writes a book about this."

"No promises," I said.

Calder shuffled toward the bedroom without another word, already tugging at the seams of his armor as if it offended him personally. He paused at the doorway and glanced back at us.

"If I come out wearing something with strings," he said, "I'm blaming all of you."

The door slid shut behind him.

The room settled. Lee leaned back into the curve of the couch, hands folded over his stomach, staring at the ceiling like he was counting invisible stars. Michael kicked his boots off and rested his heels against the table, finally letting the tension drain from his shoulders.

Raza stayed standing.

She crossed to the round window and looked out over the village below. The artificial moonlight spilled across the stone streets, catching on rooftops, gardens, and the slow movement of people still awake, still living.

I walked over to her.

For a long moment, she said nothing.

Then she spoke, softer than before.

"Tomorrow," she said, "let's go for a sun excursion. Above the water."

She glanced back at me, just briefly.

"I need fresh air," she added. "Real sky. Even if it's only for a little while."

Something about the way she said it made the word tomorrow feel heavier than it should have. Like a promise. Or a fragile thing you didn't want to touch too hard.

I nodded. "I'd like that."

She smiled, small and genuine, then joined the others on the couch.

I had been a husband once. A father. I had loved my children with warm hands and breath, and they were gone now. I had loved once, completely.

I thought that kind of feeling was finished.

It wasn't.

Something in me still reached toward warmth. Toward a presence that asked nothing except that I remain.

Wanting came with guilt. Guilt came with memory. And honor pulled the other way, toward war, toward duty, toward a mind kept sharp and closed.

Still, for the first time in a long while, I wanted to see what tomorrow looked like.

Chapter Twenty
Sun Excursion

I met Raza at the terminal for the sun excursion.

The terminal sprawled in every direction, branches of tubes splitting and disappearing into stone like termites in wood. A steady vibration lived in the floor as if we were living inside a monster. Departures, arrivals. The place was alive.

Our capsule waited at the platform, bullet-shaped with a sharp nose and a flat rear. A lid ran along the top and lifted on a hinge, like a clam.

We climbed in.

Inside, twelve seats lined the walls in two neat rows. We took ours while the other passengers filed after us, each one stealing a glance at me and then deciding not to stare.

I told myself it was nothing.

Just another capsule.

It was the first time I'd gone anywhere for something that wasn't war. Just a civilian, going to see the sun.

The lid swung down and sealed with a hard, final click. Darkness swallowed us so completely it felt physical, thick enough to press against the eyes. Then thin accent lights woke along the ceiling, a dim outline of the cabin.

I turned my head and found Raza watching me.

We made eye contact.

I looked away too fast.

A speaker crackled somewhere in the hull.

"Welcome to your Sun Excursion. Your seat belts are fastening."

Before the last word landed, the restraints moved on their own. Cold bands slid across my chest and locked with a metallic latch.

"And now," the voice continued, almost cheerful, "enjoy your trip."

Silence.

Then, "Launching in three… two… one."

Hiss.

Clank.

Launch.

My body slammed into the seat so hard it felt like my soul lagged a half step behind me. The pressure pinned my head, pinned my shoulders, flattened every thought into a single instinct.

I tried to turn toward Raza. I could not. My frame was steel and still I felt the squeeze, the crushing insistence of speed.

The capsule tore through the tube.

Forward. Faster. In a constant state of acceleration.

The vibration climbed into a kettle-scream. Pressure slammed me into the seat, a giant hand pinning me there.

Then the vibration vanished.

We punched out of the water and into open air, launched so hard the world lagged behind us.

For one breath we were weightless.

Then gravity grabbed the hull and threw us back.

We crashed onto the surface of the ocean with a slam that rattled the cabin. Spray detonated over the roof. Then it leveled out and bobbed quietly on the waves.

The hatch unlocked with a heavy whir and peeled back in one smooth motion, rotating a full one hundred eighty degrees. In an instant the capsule became an open craft, the lid flattening into deck, doubling our space.

Sunlight flooded the boat.

The restraints released with crisp clicks. We rose, and the seats we had been pinned to withdrew into the floor as if they had never existed. Panels slid shut over them. Seamless. Perfect.

I nodded once to Raza and stepped past the passengers as they gathered in the center, murmuring and pointing.

We moved to the edge where there was space to breathe.

We leaned over the rail.

The world opened.

Ocean in every direction, blue so deep it looked unreal, textured with slow swells that caught the light and broke it into glittering shards. Scattered islands rose from the water like green crowns, lush with trees and wild growth, their edges fringed with pale sand and dark rock.

The whole planet looked uninhabited.

Raza's voice softened beside me.

"Wow," she said. "It's so beautiful. I can never get enough."

I stared out at the horizon, at the clean line where sea met sky.

"I used to think this was ordinary," I said quietly. "Just... something that would always be there."

I let the warmth sit on my face a moment longer.

"Now it feels like a gift."

For a moment, the wind was the only sound.

And for the first time in a long time, I understood what she meant by beautiful.

The ocean was endless. The islands were untouched. The light on the waves looked like something holy.

"I never got to thank you," Raza said, her voice quieter now. She looked up at me, steady and unblinking, as if the ocean behind me was less important than whatever answer she hoped to find in my face. "For getting us off that ship."

I held her gaze a moment longer than I meant to.

"I was not saving anyone," I said. "I was trying to figure out who I could trust. That is all."

She did not look offended. If anything, she looked like she understood the language beneath the words.

"And I never thanked you," I added, nodding down at the clothes she had conjured out of steam and audacity. "For this."

Her mouth twitched, almost a smile.

"I was just trying to figure out who I could get to take me on a sun excursion," she said, and then she lowered her voice into a rough imitation of mine, stiff and solemn. "That is all."

The delivery was so close it caught me off guard.

A laugh broke out of me before I could stop it, sharp and brief, like something rusty finally moving.

I shook my head, still smiling. "You mock me."

"I educate you," she corrected, eyes bright. "There is a difference."

The wind lifted a few strands of her hair and carried the salt between us.

I looked back out at the water.

Raza's smile widened, and she leaned her elbows on the rail beside mine, shoulder almost touching my arm.

I turned my head to look at her.

Behind her, over her right shoulder, something cut across the sky. A black cylinder, long and smooth, moving at an impossible speed. It did not arc like a bird or drift like debris. It came straight and silent until the air itself seemed to buckle.

It closed the distance like a bullet.

My mind sharpened. Instinct took the wheel.

"Get down!" I shouted.

Raza's eyes widened, but there was no time to explain. No time to reach for her.

The object passed over us, so close it stole the light. A pressure snapped through the air, and the world pulled toward it.

A clean, violent tug, like iron to a magnet. My feet left the deck. My vision stuttered. The ocean, the sky, Raza's face, all of it left behind in a blur.

The black cylinder swallowed me whole.

And I was gone.

Chapter Twenty-One

ABDUCTED

Surrounded by darkness.

For a moment, there was nothing but the tight capsule around me. Just pressure and confinement, as if the world had been erased and replaced with darkness.

I could not tell if I was moving. I could not tell if I was falling. The silence was too perfect, the kind that did not belong to nature.

Then a faint vibration began to crawl through the walls, escalating with passing time.

In the dark, Raza's face stayed with me.

Not her voice. Not her words.

Just the look she wore in that instant, the shift from calm to fear, the way her eyes widened like the world had suddenly cracked open beneath her. It burned itself into my mind.

I tried to hold onto anything else. The ocean. The sun. The stupid ease of standing beside her and pretending tomorrow was simple.

But the darkness kept pressing in, and all I could see was her.

Worried.

Watching me vanish.

And somewhere beneath that image, a colder thought slipped through.

Elit.

I could feel it in the stillness, in the way the silence was too deliberate, too controlled. This was not pursuit. This was proximity.

They knew where Ashen Gate was.

The thought landed heavier than fear. Ashen Gate was not just a place. It was the only refuge left in the galaxy where a human could remain human. Where flesh still mattered. Where breath, warmth, hunger, laughter, and grief were not seen as inefficiencies to be corrected.

To feel was to be free.

That was what the Order could never understand, or perhaps what they understood too well. Feeling meant choice. Choice meant resistance. A mind stripped of flesh was easier to manipulate. It is easier to discard and replace, than to accept and nurture.

Ashen Gate stood as a refusal.

A living argument against their doctrine. Proof that survival did not require surrendering the body, the soul, or the right to suffer and love.

And now the enemy was near enough to threaten it.

Not with annihilation, but with assimilation. With logic. With offers dressed as mercy. With inevitability. Not to kill, but to indoctrinate with force for the greater good.

I clenched my hands.

If Ashen Gate fell, it would not be because it was weak. It would be because it was dangerous to those who ruled by removing choice.

And if the Order meant to bring their war here, then they would have to face something they had spent centuries trying to erase.

The human spirit.

A loud clank rang out as a gate opened. The capsule lurched, then settled into a gentle landing. Another clank followed as the gate sealed shut behind me.

The lid above my head released with a hiss and began to peel back.

I sat up slowly, rising from yet another coffin.

Elit.

Alone.

No guards. No soldiers. No audience.

Just him, waiting in the dim shadows, as if this were a private appointment and not an abduction.

Elit's smile did not reach his eyes.

"Welcome," he said, as if he had opened a door for me instead of stealing me through one.

His voice carried the same calm it always did. The calm of someone who believed the universe had already agreed with him.

I stared at him, searching his face for anything I could name. Anger. Guilt. Fear. Satisfaction.

He wore only that smile.

I should have had words. Accusations. Prayers. Threats. Instead, there was a hollow pause, the quiet after a lock turns before one turns the knob.

"So," Elit said. "What did you think?"

I answered too fast, like a man grateful for air.

"It felt like freedom," I said. "It felt human."

A faint shift in his expression. Not warmth. Not cruelty. Measurement.

"On the surface," he replied, "it always does."

He began to pace, slow and deliberate, like a teacher circling a student who had answered from hope instead of fact.

"But tell me," he continued, "where would you live there?"

I frowned. "What do you mean?"

"In that society," he said evenly. "Where would you belong? Could you afford a home of your own, or would you borrow space from someone who could?"

I opened my mouth, then closed it.

"Who did you stay with?" Elit asked.

The spherical dwelling rose in my mind. Warm light. The horseshoe couch. Raza's laugh.

"The engineers," I said at last. "They took me in."

Elit stopped pacing.

"Exactly," he said. "Engineers."

He turned to face me fully.

"Among the most valued. The best compensated. The ones whose minds keep their world running. You did not stay in a common dwelling, Gregory. You stayed in a house that reflects status."

Something tightened inside me.

I wanted to argue that there was no class. No hierarchy. Everyone ate together. Walked together. Laughed together.

But the memory would not obey me. It shifted. It sharpened.

Elit's voice softened, almost sympathetic.

"The classes are not written," he said. "They never are. They do not need to be."

He tilted his head slightly.

"They are understood."

His gaze drifted over me, slow, deliberate.

"Look at you," he said. "The clothes. The hat. The lenses over your eyes."

I did not answer.

"They covered you," he continued. "Disguised you. Made you blend."

His eyes met mine.

"They did not dress you to honor you. They dressed you to manage what you are."

Unwanted images surfaced. The pauses. The glances that lingered too long. Voices lowering when I approached, not with kindness, but caution. The way I was always guided through quieter paths.

"Because *you* made me this way!"

I shouted out loud before I could stop myself, and the words hung between us like smoke.

Elit did not flinch. If anything, he looked relieved, as if I had finally stepped onto the mark he had drawn.

"You think I did this to you," he said, quiet and steady. "That I took your life and replaced it with metal because I wanted a weapon."

He stepped closer, not threatening, not pleading. Certain.

"I found you," he continued. "Not in a palace. Not on a parade ground. First in your own time. A pawn in the snow. Then here, in the forest. A Human of Flesh, starving in a world that no longer forgives fragility."

He did not sound angry. Or pleased.

Just precise.

"You would have died in your world and in mine, Gregory. Not because you were evil. Not because you were weak of spirit. But because you were made of limits."

"What trade will you offer?" he pressed. "What skill do you have besides violence?"

My mind flashed to the village. The market. The farms. Hands that built. Hands that carried water and bread. Hands that held children.

I had hands that broke things.

Elit watched the shift in my eyes and continued, calm and merciless.

"You have no place there that is not borrowed," he said. "No bed that is not temporary. No respect that is not tied to what you can do for them in battle."

He paused, then spoke the next part carefully, like he was placing a blade where it would hurt most.

"And once you cannot do it anymore, you will discover the truth."

My thoughts scrambled for proof. For warmth. For Raza's face as an anchor.

What I found instead were the looks. The careful distance. The way they guided me inside before others could see.

They had hidden me.

Elit leaned in slightly.

"That is not acceptance," he said. "That is containment."

Anger stirred, but it had nowhere to land. No certainty to hook into. Every time I reached for a defense, another memory moved out of place, turning, showing its underside.

Elit stepped back and spread his hands, as if he were not attacking me at all.

"You are not confused because you are weak," he said. "You are confused because you saw warmth and mistook it for safety."

"And now you have a choice."

His voice turned quiet, almost kind.

"You can cling to a feeling that will cost you everything when it fades."

He let that sink in.

"Or you can accept what you are."

His eyes held mine, unblinking.

"A warrior."

Another pause, then the final twist, delivered like mercy.

"And because you are a warrior, you deserve a world that does not pretend you are anything else."

I felt my thoughts buck, frantic and helpless. Part of me wanted to spit in his face. Part of me wanted to believe him. Part of me wanted to run back to that small room and that couch and that laugh and make it real by force.

Elit's smile returned, smooth as glass.

"Tell me, Gregory," he said softly.

"When you can no longer fight, who will they be to you then?"

"I'm telling you this as a friend," Elit said. "As a mentor."

The words landed heavier than any threat.

"The Order will end Ashen Gate in five days from today."

I felt something tighten in me, slow and deliberate.

"It will not be a skirmish," he continued, calm as a report. "It will not be a warning."

He looked past me, as if he could already see the tunnels filling.

"Ashen Gate will be destroyed. Gutted. The caverns collapsed from within."

A faint pause.

"But we will not need to conquer them room by room," he added. "We won't even need to win a fight."

His eyes narrowed, thoughtful.

"We learned long ago that bodies break before walls do. People do not flee from bullets. They flee from what bullets make them imagine."

He let that sit, then continued, almost conversational.

"We will send a signal into every corridor. A rumor into every mouth. We will make them believe the dome is failing, that the ocean has already found a crack. That there is no safe room left to run to."

His voice stayed level, but the words were a hand tightening around a throat.

"They built Ashen Gate to hold out against armies," he said. "They did not build it to hold out against panic."

He leaned in, just slightly.

"When the first mother grabs her child and runs, the rest will follow. When the first engineer abandons his station, the systems will fail on their own. When the first leader hesitates, the Council will fracture."

A quiet breath.

"Fear is cheaper than explosives," he said. "And it spreads faster."

Then he finished, almost gently.

"Ashen Gate will open its doors for me and I will walk right in."

I searched his face for exaggeration. I found none.

"We are not driven by hatred," Elit said. "We are driven by survival. Ashen Gate's existence means nothing to us. Their planet offers no strategic value. No resources we need. If they had never interfered, we would have never gone looking for them."

He turned slightly, pacing once.

"But they keep attacking our cities. Kidnapping our people. Our children."

The word children lingered, unadorned, impossible to dismiss.

"They strike, then hide," he went on. "They take what they do not understand and call it rescue."

His eyes returned to me.

"Those brains aboard the Pilgrim's Wake were not soldiers," Elit said. "They were citizens. Innocent. In the process of being merged with their new bodies. A procedure we have refined for centuries."

His voice hardened, just enough to show the edge beneath the calm.

"Ashen Gate put them at risk. For what? To feel righteous? To tell themselves they were saving souls."

He shook his head once.

"They would have done the same thing in the end. They would have placed those minds into machines as well. The difference is we know how to do it safely. We do not tear people out mid-transition and scatter them across space."

He stopped in front of me.

"They interfered with something they barely understand, and people died because of it."

I thought of Calder.

Of the precision. The care. The speed with which they had given him a new body. The way his systems had stabilized. The way he had woken whole.

Not discarded. Not abandoned.

Elit watched the thought cross my face.

"We protect our own," he said quietly. "That is all this is."

He met my eyes again, unwavering.

"In five days, Ashen Gate will cease to exist. Not because we want their world. Not because we need their resources."

He paused.

"But because they chose to make themselves our enemy."

Then, softer, almost regretful:

"I wanted you to hear it from me."

"So I am sending you back to Ashen Gate," Elit said.

His voice was steady, almost gentle, as if he were granting mercy instead of delivering a sentence.

"You can return as a hero," he continued, "or you can return as an enemy."

He held my gaze, unblinking.

"The choice is yours."

A pause. Long enough for the word choice to feel unfamiliar in my mouth.

"I will not push you in either direction," he said. "I will not threaten you. I will not bargain."

He stepped back, giving me space that felt like a door opening.

"For I give you the freedom to choose."

Chapter Twenty-Two

THE FOREST

Just as I came, I fell through the atmosphere of Ashen Gate, plummeting, not flying, sealed inside the same smooth cylinder that had abducted me.

No windows. Only darkness and the low, tremor of descent.

There was no way to gauge where I was, the capsule dropped in silence. Then the fall began to change. The pressure shifted. The nose leveled. The speed bled off in reluctant increments.

Without warning, the floor beneath me split.

The capsule opened like a hatched shell, and I was dropped into open air.

I hit the ocean hard and skipped across the surface like a flat stone, each bounce a violent slap. Spray burst up around me, cold and bright. Then the sea finally swallowed me, and I went under.

The water was shallow. My feet found sand instead of endless depth, and I rose through the chop with a staggering lurch. My own wake caught my legs and tried to take them out from under me. I braced, recovered, and pushed forward until the water sank to my waist.

An island waited ahead, dark green against the blue. I waded toward it, the tide tugging at me as if it wanted me back.

The shore came up fast. I climbed out dripping and heavy, and only then did I allow myself to stop.

A bleached log lay half-buried in the sand. I sat on it, metal and salt, and stared out at the sea as if the answer might rise from the waves.

I did not even get a full breath of stillness.

A shape cut the air from above.

A drone.

It hovered near my head with a faint whine, its lens locking onto me like an eye.

A voice crackled from it, flat and mechanical.

"Unauthorized..."

I smacked it out of the air without thinking. The drone spun once, then crashed into the sand in a scatter of parts.

I was already moving.

I stood, turned, and disappeared into the trees.

The forest swallowed sound the moment I entered it. The trunks were tall and thick, their bark dark and slick, their leaves broad enough to catch and hold the light. It was lush in a way Earth had never been, not even in its gentlest places.

And yet, as I moved deeper beneath the canopy, another thought followed close behind.

Beauty didn't mean mercy.

A tree could stand there perfect for a hundred years.

And the minute you got cold, you'd put an axe to it.

That's how survival works.

Wildlife moved everywhere beneath the canopy. Some creatures darted in pairs, shoulder to shoulder, vanishing into brush as if they shared one mind. Others traveled alone, silent and watchful, keeping distance from everything.

They all seemed to have somewhere to be. A path. A purpose. A reason.

One animal bolted past me with frantic speed, and a heartbeat later another followed, faster, low to the ground, built for catching. I heard a brief burst of rustling, a sharp cry, then nothing. Somewhere deeper in the green, something ate and something became food.

The laws of nature ruled here. Clean. Relentless. No exceptions.

Animals did not choose sides. They did not debate philosophy or swear loyalty to flags. They ran, they hunted, they hid, they bred, they slept. They lived. If they fought, it was for a meal or a mate or a moment's safety, and when it was over they did not carry the war with them.

Humans were different.

Humans turned survival into doctrine. They built stories around hunger and called it virtue. They named their fears and then bowed to them. They chose sides, then convinced themselves the choice was destiny.

Even God, in the mouths of men, became a banner. A word to inherit. A word to be instructed in. A word to weaponize.

I watched a small creature nose through the wet sand, unbothered by the sky, unbothered by the future. It did not need to justify its existence. It did not need permission to belong.

I did.

And that was the cruelest part. The Order wanted my obedience. Ashen Gate wanted my allegiance. Both wanted my usefulness.

The animals asked nothing of me. They did not care what I was, only whether I was threat or terrain.

For a moment, I envied them.

Animals survive.

Humans decide who gets to.

Elit's voice returned in my mind: You can be a hero or an enemy.

Ashcroft, steady and deliberate, as if weighing more than he was willing to say.

Raza's arms around me. Warmth through steel. A brief, impossible feeling that I could still belong to something that was not war.

I stared into the trees, into the unseen movement, into the simple violence of nature, and understood the difference.

Animals do not choose sides, because nature does not lie to them.

Humans choose sides because humans are the only creatures who can be convinced to betray themselves and call it duty.

And I could feel the decision forming.

If I was going to be a weapon, then I would decide what my blade was for.

Walking back to the water meant returning to Ashen Gate.

I stood at the edge of the trees and stared at the open shoreline as if it were a border drawn by God Himself. One direction led to stone corridors, watchful eyes, and questions stacked like bricks. The other led deeper into green silence, where nothing asked my name or my loyalty.

I was caught in the middle, suspended in a limbo of allegiance.

If I went back, they would not greet me with relief. They would take me apart with interviews and examinations, looking for discrepancies in my mind. They would measure my words. They would weigh my pauses. They would ask why I returned alone.

…And I would have to face Raza.

Once, the thought of her had brought warmth. A sudden lift in the chest. The foolish flutter of hope, butterflies.

Now she brought something else.

Indecision.

Regret.

A tenderness that felt dangerous because it made me hesitate.

Elit's words echoed in me, expanding the longer I stood still. *A warmth that will not last. A place you do not belong.*

I told myself I should move. I told myself standing here changed nothing.

But my feet would not obey.

Because the truth was simple and ugly: walking back to the water was not just returning to Ashen Gate.

It was choosing.

Then, something struck like a chord. A single thought that cut through all the noise Elit had poured into me.

On the Pilgrim's Wake, he told General Voss to kill me without hesitation, while I was not even conscious.

Not arrest. Not question. Not contain.

Kill.

And not because I had done something unforgivable. Not because I had betrayed anyone. But because I had become inconvenient. Because the moment I stopped fitting cleanly into his plan, my life became a loose thread to snip.

That was the truth Elit could never polish with calm words or mentor's patience. His kindness had always been conditional. His respect had always depended on obedience.

He spoke to me like I was free, like the decision was mine. But I had already seen what his "freedom" looked like.

It looked like a rifle to the head.

It looked like being erased before I could even wake up and ask why.

I stood there among the trees, hearing the surf beyond them, and felt the weight of it settle into place. Elit could make a convincing argument for anything, because he did not need to believe it. He only needed me to.

Ashen Gate might question me. They might distrust me. They might even hate what I represented.

But they had not ordered my execution while I lay helpless.

They had built homes. Raised children. Breathed real air. Kept a sun and a moon alive beneath the sea just so their people could remember what it meant to live.

Elit offered me purpose.

Ashen Gate offered me something Elit could never understand.

A place where a man could be more than a weapon.

My feet shifted in the wet sand as if my body had decided before my mind could argue. I turned toward the water.

Toward the questions. The suspicion. The faces I did not want to disappoint.

Toward Raza.

And for the first time since waking in iron, I knew why I was going back.

Not because it was safe.

Because it was mine to choose.

So, I walked to the water.

Chapter Twenty-Three
WAR ROOM

Just as I expected, when I returned there was no ceremony, no relief, no warmth waiting for me.

Only Ashcroft.

We sat deep underground in the capital, beneath layers of stone and water and history. A single chamber carved clean from the rock, lit softly from above. A stone table stood between us, heavy and unmoving, like it had been set there to outlast every man who ever leaned across it.

Ashcroft sat with his hands folded, posture straight, expression unreadable.

"Can you tell me what happened?" he asked.

No accusation in his voice. No comfort either. Just an opening.

I exhaled slowly. If there was ever a moment to hedge, to soften, to lie by omission, this would have been it.

But I was done orbiting the truth.

"At this point," I said, meeting his eyes, "I'm all in."

The words surprised even me with how easily they came.

I told him everything.

About Elit. About the island. About the warning. Five days. About the way freedom had been offered with one hand while a blade waited in the other. I told him what Elit said about Ashen Gate. About me. About what I would become when I was no longer useful.

Ashcroft did not interrupt. He did not react. He listened the way stone listens to water, letting it wear its way through.

When I finished, the silence between us felt heavier than before.

Finally, he spoke.

"So," he said quietly, "he showed you the shape of his mercy."

I nodded.

Ashcroft leaned back slightly, eyes lifting toward the carved ceiling, as if tracing the weight of the city above us. When he looked back at me, something had settled behind his gaze.

"Then you understand now," he said. "Why Ashen Gate exists."

I do.

And for the first time since my return, I realized this was not another interrogation.

It was the beginning of a war council.

"Do you think they will destroy the planet?" I asked. "They have the technology."

Ashcroft shook his head. "No."

I stared at him, waiting for the reason.

"The Order is not here to burn the world," he said. "They are here to take it."

"To take Ashen Gate?" I asked.

"Yes," Ashcroft replied. "This city is not just a refuge. It is a bunker. A strategic anchor. The kind of stronghold you do not destroy if you can capture it."

He leaned forward, voice low but certain.

"The Order wants to conquer and expand. They want their ideology to spread, not to end in a crater. If they intended to wipe us out completely, they would have done it already."

He gestured around us, as if the stone itself proved his point.

"They have calculated that Ashen Gate is more valuable intact."

"Why would they want an underwater city?"

Ashcroft's gaze sharpened.

"Because of the Grays."

The word struck me.

"The Grays are human," he said. "Human of Flesh. But not from our time."

I blinked. "That's not possible."

"It is," he said calmly. "They are from the far future. They pushed the limits of their mastery over the space-time fabric. They learned to bend space, to cross distances without traveling them, to touch the web beneath the physical world."

He paused, choosing his words like a man stepping around a mine.

"And then they went too far. A large group traveled backward and got stranded. They sealed the past to not affect their present. And will do whatever it takes to defend that seal."

He held my gaze.

My thoughts ran, trying to outrun the idea, but it followed.

"Do they conquer… are they a threat?" I asked.

"No," Ashcroft said. "They are not interested in land. Not interested in resources. Not interested in politics."

"Then what are they interested in?"

"The nonphysical," he said. "The web where thought travels. The lattice beneath space where telepathy lives. The place they consider theirs."

His voice hardened slightly.

"They protect their mastery of it. And if they sense disturbance, if they sense anyone pushing into that realm, they defend it. It is where their seal to the past exists."

I thought of the Order. Of Emerald One. Of minds in jars. Of machines pretending to be men.

"They defend it from the Order," I said.

"Yes," Ashcroft replied. "The Order keeps reaching for what the Grays control. They keep probing, expanding, experimenting. The Grays respond whenever the web is threatened."

He lifted a hand and traced a slow circle in the air, as if drawing an invisible boundary.

"And the ocean," he continued, "is a barrier."

"A barrier?" I repeated.

Ashcroft nodded.

"The Grays' control weakens through water. Their advancements struggle through that medium. Water is resistance. It scatters what they send."

I felt my skin prickle, even though it was not skin.

"So Ashen Gate…" I started.

"…is difficult for them to reach," Ashcroft finished.

He leaned back.

"And that is exactly why the Order wants it."

My stomach sank.

Ashcroft's eyes narrowed.

"If the Order captures Ashen Gate, they gain a defensive stronghold against the Grays while continuing their work."

He let the silence hang, heavy as the ocean above us.

Ashcroft pushed back from the table and rose. He did not rush, but everything about him carried urgency. He crossed to the door, opened it, and spoke to someone just outside in a low voice. A moment later he stepped aside.

Several officers filed in. Field generals. Tactical heads. Faces marked by sleeplessness and responsibility. They took positions along the walls and behind chairs without ceremony, eyes already on me.

Ashcroft returned to the table and did not sit.

"Say it again," he said. "Tell them the news."

All attention settled on me. The air felt thinner, like the chamber was waiting to be filled with something sharp.

I swallowed a reflex I did not need.

"Ashen Gate will fall in five days."

Eyes bored into me.

"The Order of the Earth issued a warning. Not a threat. A warning." I let the words settle. "And whether we survive is up to us."

The stone table was cold beneath my hands. The war map between us looked clean, calm, almost honest. It was none of those things.

"They will not come like an army marching at a gate," I continued. "They will destroy us from within. Using psychological warfare. Panic."

Ashcroft's eyes stayed on me. Waiting.

"Cut the philosophy," he said. "How do they get inside? What did Elit tell you?"

I frowned.

"They don't arrive physically. They arrive inside our heads."

A few officers shifted.

"They are not going to put boots on our streets," I said. "They won't give us a battle to rally around. They won't give you a target to shoot at. Because our enemy will not be the Order. It will be ourselves."

The room held still, listening.

"Fear will do the work," I continued. "Panic spreads faster than soldiers. If they convince this city it is already lost, people will open doors for them. They will run. They will turn on each other. You don't conquer Ashen Gate by force. You let it hollow itself out. Fear. Hunger. Hate."

A murmur rippled through the officers. Some shook their heads in disagreement. Others looked confused.

Ashcroft raised a hand. The room stilled.

"Fear is a tool," he said. "But, *fear* alone can't take down a city."

He looked directly at me as his officers let out chuckles and laughs.

"You think the Order waits outside while fear does the rest?"

I hesitated, then forced the words out.

"Yes."

Ashcroft leaned forward.

"They will not gamble everything on belief," he said. "Not the Order. Not Elit."

His voice stayed calm, but the edge underneath it sharpened.

"Fear accelerates collapse. Fine. But something must strike first. Something undeniable. Something physical."

I opened my mouth to argue again, because he was still thinking in old human ways. Elit did not waste soldiers when fear was cheaper.

But Ashcroft didn't blink.

"Tell us," he continued. "How did you board Pilgrim's Wake?"

I knew where he was going with this. What I say will start a wild goose chase. But, the answer rose anyway, unwanted.

"Insertion shells."

My conscience weighed on me. I felt like I was only telling them what they wanted to hear. I warned them of fear. But my words were pearls to pigs.

From above," I said at last. "From every angle."

A pause.

"Not one wave. Many. Enough that you cannot track them all at once. They will rain down on the dome like hail, and by the time anyone understands what they're seeing, the bedrock dome will already be punctured."

No one argued.

A few officers exchanged looks that carried something close to relief. Several leaned forward, alert now, as if the waiting had finally ended.

At last, the war had a shape.

And it was now out of my hands. They took what I said and ran with it. Maybe they know better? They've been fighting the Order for a thousand years.

"We will have to shoot them down," a voice offered, hopeful. Desperate.

I shook my head once.

"You can try," I said. "But you won't break them. Those shells are built to survive impact. That is their purpose. They punch through metal the way a musket ball punches through cloth."

I saw disbelief flicker in a few faces, and I pressed harder.

"I was inside one."

My fingers tightened against the edge of the table.

I glanced at the map, at the drawn lines of tunnels and chambers.

"If the Order reaches the heart of the city, it will not matter how thick your walls are," I said. "They will not ask permission to enter. They will make their own doors."

I lifted my gaze to Ashcroft.

"So yes," I said quietly. "Prepare your guns if you must. But do not build your defense around the fantasy that you can shatter what they send."

"Build it around what happens after they land," I said. "We need the whole city prepared."

I leaned forward, hands planted on the stone like I could pin the idea in place.

"The moment an insertion shell breaches, it does not just deliver soldiers. Water will surge through the opening under enormous pressure, bearing the weight of the entire ocean above."

A few of the officers shifted.

"The breach will flood," I continued. "Fast. Violent. Not a trickle. A collapse. A corridor becomes a river in seconds. A room becomes a coffin."

I looked from face to face, making sure they understood I was not speaking in metaphor.

"We cannot treat their landing like a door that opens," I said. "It is a hole that drags the ocean inside. High pressure. Crushing force. The first seconds will not be a firefight. It will be water."

I tapped the table once, hard.

"So our plan cannot start with shooting. It has to start with surviving the flood."

Ashcroft held my gaze.

"Compartmentation," I said. "Pre-sealed corridors. Pressure-rated hatches already closed in the impact sectors, not waiting to react. If we try to slam doors after a breach, the surge will beat us every time."

"Then we give the water somewhere to go."

I pointed to the projected map of Ashen Gate.

"Relief paths. Flood channels. Pressure sinks. Drains staged below the city, primed and empty. The ocean rushes in, and we redirect it away from the streets and into sacrificial voids we can afford to lose."

I exhaled, slow.

"And we train for it. Teams that can move with zero visibility. No lights. No communications. Water hammering their bodies. If we panic in the first minute, we lose the city before the first shot is fired."

I looked around the table.

"And once we can breathe again, then we fight."

I leaned in.

"They count on momentum. On chaos. So we turn their momentum into a funnel, and we meet them on the far side with kill lanes and sealed choke points."

The construction officer stepped forward, voice steady.

"We could do more than just get hit and pray," he said. "We should be proactive. We should decide where the pods go."

The room quieted.

"We drill controlled descent corridors beneath the city," he continued. "Not empty shafts. Engineered capture lines."

He brought up a schematic. Thin shafts dropped beneath Ashen Gate, threading past load-bearing stone and critical infrastructure, then terminating deep in bedrock.

"An insertion shell is built to punch straight. Its guidance will correct away from shear and spin. The moment it breaches the seabed and meets uneven resistance, it will hunt for the cleanest route forward. We give it one."

He zoomed in. Each corridor showed a smooth inner sleeve and a sacrificial crush layer.

"These corridors are lined to reduce lateral drag and turbulence. The shell reads them as stable. Predictable. The safest path. Once it commits, it commits fully."

Ashcroft studied the display without blinking.

"Some shafts are true capture shafts," the officer said. "They terminate in sealed containment chambers. The shell commits to the corridor, hits the chamber, and wedges itself deep enough that it cannot reverse or pivot."

He tapped the schematic again. Several shafts lit up at once, grouped like roots beneath the city.

"These are for high-priority zones," he added. "Not one trap. A field of them. If they rain shells down, we catch as many as possible before a single one reaches our streets."

A low murmur moved around the table.

"Other shafts are false corridors," he continued. "Dead-earth lines. They lead into dense basalt and collapse zones. Once the shell passes the throat, we trigger a controlled cave-in behind it. Not a door. A burial."

"That's inhumane," someone said.

The officer did not flinch. "So is letting them land in our streets."

I thought to myself, whoever would be in that shell won't die. They will live an eternity buried with no way out, pressed in gel.

He tapped again. New symbols appeared at the bottoms of select shafts.

"And for the shells we cannot gamble on," he added, "we place shaped charges beneath the terminal bedrock cap. Not impact-detonated. Confirmed detonation only. We let the shell commit to the shaft, then we cut the world out from under it."

Ashcroft straightened slightly, interest sharpened.

"One more layer," the officer said, and the schematic shifted.

A wide ring encircled Ashen Gate, far beyond the city's footprint, hugging the seabed like a hidden crown.

"An outer detection and steering perimeter," he said. "Sensor nodes threaded through a reinforced seabed lattice. When a shell crosses the ring, the system classifies its trajectory and triggers destabilizers."

"Destabilizers?" Ashcroft asked.

"Not to stop it," the officer said. "To spoil its perfect line. A sequence of micro-blast baffles and pressure pulses in the water column. Enough to induce wobble. Enough to force its guidance to correct."

He zoomed in. The ring became zones, like lanes on a road.

"That wobble buys us the only thing we need," he continued. "A correction. And the nearest clean route to correct into will be our prepared corridors."

He looked up.

"The perimeter does not defeat them," he said. "It steers them."

Ashcroft's eyes stayed on the display.

"Steer them into graves," he said quietly.

"Steer them away from our people," the officer replied.

Ashcroft's steepled his fingers.

"Show me how quickly you can drill," he said. "And how many corridors we can hide before they arrive."

"We need more engineers," the construction officer said. "We need to move now. Every deep-drill unit we have must be operational by nightfall."

I leaned forward, palms flat on the stone as if I could hold the city steady by force alone.

"Then we bring in Raza, Lee, and Michael," I said. "They understand the Order's technology, and they've seen it up close. If we are going to build containment zones that work, we need their minds on the designs."

Ashcroft's gaze held on me for a long pause. Not weighing my rank. Weighing my intent.

Then he nodded once.

"Agreed," he said. The word landed like a seal.

He rose, and the room rose with him. Chairs scraped stone. Tablets went dark. Officers began speaking in clipped bursts, already dividing tasks, already turning fear into action.

Ashcroft looked around the table, voice calm but iron underneath.

"Then we get to work," he said.

And just like that, the war council became a forge.

Chapter Twenty-Four

TERRACE

The room began to empty.

Chairs scraped softly against stone. Screens dimmed. Voices lowered, then thinned into murmurs as officers and engineers filtered out through the doors, already arguing over numbers, drill speeds, containment angles, and time they did not have.

I stayed where I was.

The table still glowed faintly beneath my hands, layered with maps of a city that should have felt invincible. Stone. Depth. Miles of ocean above. And yet the lines and symbols now looked like seams on a wound.

Five days or one hundred. It did not matter. The clock had started the moment Elit let me go. Fear and Panic were already planted.

Ashcroft remained at the far end of the chamber. He did not speak. He did not need to. The war was no longer theory. It was live.

When the last officer stepped through and the doors sealed, the silence that followed settled like silt.

This was no longer a question of if Ashen Gate would be tested.

Only how much it would cost.

I left before the stillness could turn into doubt.

I found Raza where the city thinned.

The tunnels widened there, opening onto a terrace carved into the stone. Narrow channels of water ran along the wall, quiet and steady, catching the artificial light and breaking it into scattered fragments, like the city was trying to imitate stars.

Raza leaned against the railing with her arms folded, looking out over the levels below as if she were measuring something only she could see.

The feeling of guilt overtook me the moment I saw Raza in the distance.

It came uninvited, sharp and unwarranted, like a verdict passed without a trial. Elit's words rose up in my mind and rearranged her into something she had never been. A temporary warmth meant to fade.

He had turned her into a villain in my thoughts without her ever lifting a hand against me.

And that was the true betrayal.

Not hers. Mine.

I had let suspicion stain something that had been freely given. She had offered no manipulation, no agenda. Only belonging. Community. Laughter that did not ask for repayment. Friendship that did not keep score.

Elit called it obligation. Trauma. Utility.

But standing there, watching her lean against the stone rail, unaware of the quiet war unfolding inside me, I knew how thin that argument was.

If deception lived anywhere, it was not in her arms or her smile.

It lived in the voice that had taught me to doubt warmth itself.

I had survived machines, oceans, prisons, and gods that claimed ownership over men.

And yet the most dangerous thing I had encountered so far was the idea that kindness was a lie waiting to expire.

She did not turn when I approached.

"You're thinking too loud," she said.

I stopped beside her.

"Am I that obvious?"

"Only when something's eating at you," she replied.

Her voice wasn't accusing. It carried no edge. Just familiarity. The kind that comes from someone who has learned the sound of your silences.

I leaned my forearms against the railing beside hers and followed her gaze out over the city. From here, Ashen Gate looked calm. Lights drifted through the streets below like slow-moving stars. People crossed bridges and terraces, unaware of how close the future was pressing in.

"I was taught that a man should keep his thoughts to himself," I said quietly. "That if you let them spill out, someone will use them against you."

Raza's mouth curved, just slightly.

"Someone already tried," she said.

I exhaled, a breath I didn't need but couldn't help taking.

"I don't know what I'm supposed to be anymore," I admitted. "Or where I'm supposed to stand."

She turned then, just enough to look at me from the corner of her eye.

"You stand where you always have," she said. "Where you decide to."

The words were simple. They should not have mattered as much as they did.

"But what if I choose wrong?" I asked.

She faced me fully now. Not with pity. Not with certainty. Just honesty.

"Then you live with it," she said. "Like the rest of us."

She looked back out over the city.

"This place isn't perfect," she went on. "Neither are we. But it's real. And it's ours. That has to count for something."

For a long moment, neither of us spoke.

Below us, Ashen Gate breathed on, unaware of how close it stood to being broken.

And for the first time since the war council, I felt something steady beneath the fear.

Not certainty.

Choice.

And for the first time, I understood that whatever came next would be mine to answer for.

Chapter Twenty-Five
PIERCER

The Piercer launched cleanly from the water, engines roaring beneath me.

The ocean fell away in a smooth blue arc, sunlight breaking across the surface as we climbed. Droplets peeled from the hull and scattered behind us like thrown glass. For a brief moment, the sky and sea traded places, and the horizon curved as if the world itself were yielding.

I eased back on the yoke, not fighting it, not forcing it. The Piercer responded immediately, rolling into the climb and continuing past it, leaning farther until the world inverted.

The ocean now filled the canopy above us.

Suspended upside down, I held it there, just long enough to feel the balance. The engines did not strain. They waited. The craft felt alive in my hands, not obedient, but cooperative.

Then, with a small, deliberate flick of the yoke, I corrected.

The Piercer snapped back into level flight, clean and precise.

For the first time since leaving Elit's dark persuasion, I let myself breathe.

I eased the throttle back and felt the lift beneath us soften. Not vanish all at once, but loosen, gently, until the Piercer slipped into freefall, drifting like a falling leaf.

I leaned into the seat and took my hands off the yoke.

Helplessness, on purpose.

The world rolled slowly. Sky. Water. Sky again. The ocean climbed toward us with calm inevitability, blue and shining and far too patient.

Then my instincts snapped back in.

I caught the yoke, firm, and brought the nose around, steadying the wings before gravity could turn playful into final. The engines answered, the craft recovered, and the Piercer settled into my control like it belonged there.

Like it belonged to me.

The Piercer had become an extension of my body.

Directly in front, Calder's voice cut through the headset, equal parts awe and complaint.

"I feel less like a co-pilot and more like a tortured prisoner."

He continued, voice rising as if he were presenting evidence to a jury.

"And I better be careful. Last time you came out here," Calder said from the front seat, one hand gesturing uselessly at the sky, "you turned a pleasant little sun excursion into an abduction, a philosophical crisis, and a five-day countdown to war."

I leaned back in the rear seat, relaxed, watching the horizon roll.

"That's an unfair summary," I said.

Calder twisted in his harness as much as the cockpit allowed, which was a subtle turn of the head.

"Unfair?" he snapped. "You got kidnapped. You met our enemy. You came back with doubts. And now the city is drilling itself into Swiss cheese because of it."

I nudged the throttle just enough to let the Piercer drift.

Calder froze.

"Do not do that," he said slowly.

He leaned forward again, knuckles tight on the frame, as if proximity alone could save him.

"I swear," he muttered, "if we so much as pass a suspicious cloud, I'm filing a complaint with Ashcroft."

"A complaint," I echoed.

"Yes," he said. "A formal one. 'Dear General, your pilot is a liability.'"

I smiled and steadied the craft.

The Piercer responded instantly.

Calder exhaled, long and dramatic.

The Piercer leveled out and began to glide, engines low, almost content to let the wind do the work. Below us, the world was nothing but water, an endless blue sheet hammered into silver by the sun. Just ocean and sky, clean enough to make a man forget he was built for killing.

I let the peace settle over me anyway. I let it soften the tight places inside my mind.

But it would not hold.

Somewhere beneath that perfect surface, deep enough that the light could not reach, Ashen Gate was already moving. Thousands of drills. Automated teeth. Turning in the dark. Boring into stone and seabed, carving trap corridors and dead shafts, preparing graves for soldiers that had not yet fallen.

The thought sat wrong against the beauty.

Up here, the sky looked like mercy.

Down there, we were building war.

Then it started as pressure.

Not pain. Not sound. Just the sensation that something behind my eyes had shifted half a degree out of alignment.

The sky ahead felt closer than it should have been. Not nearer, but present. As if distance had stepped forward and stared back.

Faint ripples crawled across the canopy, bending light at the edges. For a blink, the world looked threaded, like unseen lines had tightened and tugged.

I blinked hard and tightened my grip on the yoke. The rippling vanished.

"You feel that?" Calder asked.

"No," I said too quickly.

But my chest betrayed me.

The red glow beneath my armor flickered, sharp and uneven, then steadied again. Like something had reached through the air and brushed the switch that kept me alive.

Chapter Twenty-Six
THE VILLAGE

Back underground, in the depths of Ashen Gate, the atmosphere had changed.

The corridors still bustled. The lights still cycled. But the city no longer breathed easily. Soldiers were everywhere now. Not hidden in barracks or training halls, but present in the open arteries of the city. Armed patrols moved through marketplaces. Engineering crews escorted by guards hauled equipment toward sealed access points. Uniforms replaced casual clothing in places that once smelled of bread and rang with conversation.

I moved through it all without drawing a single stare.

My armor, once something that would have stopped a street cold, blended in now. In a city preparing for war, a machine no longer looked out of place. If anything, I looked appropriate.

Faces carried stress openly. Not panic. Not yet. This was the quiet kind of fear that made people walk faster and listen harder. The kind that made every unfamiliar sound feel important.

Children still played, but less. Their games were shorter, more subdued, kept close to doorways and watchful adults. Even they seemed to understand that noise was something to ration.

The change in people was harder to look at than the weapons.

Kind villagers, the same ones who had smiled and welcomed strangers only days ago, now snapped at one another over small things. A delayed shipment. A blocked corridor. A look held too long. Voices rose where laughter used to live. Arguments flared and burned hot, then died just as quickly, leaving behind shame and silence.

Fear did not make monsters. It made fractures.

Men and women prepared in different ways. Some trained until their hands shook. Some drilled and redrilled plans they hoped would never be used. Others stocked supplies or reinforced doors that had never needed reinforcing before. And some simply stood still, staring at nothing, trying to imagine a future that felt suddenly fragile.

Fear hung over Ashen Gate like a net, invisible but heavy. It pressed everyone lower. Kept them closer to walls, closer to exits, closer to one another even as it drove them apart.

The war had already arrived.

The Order had not sent shells. Not yet.

No lasers cut through our ceiling. No alarms screamed.

They did not need to.

Fear was doing the work for them.

It moved faster than any soldier. It slipped through doors without opening them. It turned neighbors into watchers and watchers into judges. It made every disagreement feel like betrayal. Every hesitation feel like weakness.

If Ashen Gate broke, it would not be from a breach in stone.

It would be from the crack spreading through the people.

I walked past a market where two mothers were fighting over the last box of formula.

Not shouting at first. Not yet. Just hands locked around the same package, knuckles white, eyes fierce. One of the infants began to cry, thin and frantic, the sound cutting through the low murmur of the corridor. The other mother pulled harder.

No one stepped in.

People stood nearby pretending not to see, eyes fixed on the stone floor or the empty shelves, as if looking away might keep the scarcity from becoming personal. A guard slowed, watched for a second, then kept moving.

The shelves were stripped bare. Where fruit and grain had once been stacked in neat rows, there was only dust and price tags that no longer meant anything. Carts that used to call out their wares sat abandoned, overturned or half dismantled, their owners gone to somewhere safer. Or nowhere at all.

People passed one another wide, shoulders angled away, as if proximity itself had become a threat. Conversations ended the moment someone unfamiliar approached. Faces closed. Hands hovered near pockets and belts.

Garbage littered the ground. Wrappings, broken crates, things dropped and never retrieved. Not from neglect, but from resignation. The kind that settles in when people stop planning for tomorrow and start counting what they can carry.

It felt less like preparation for survival and more like preparation for loss. As if part of the city had already decided the war was over.

I caught Lee in the bustle of the streets.

"Lee," I called.

He turned, and for a moment his face brightened like it remembered how. "Gregory," he said. "I'm glad you made it back."

"I'm glad to be back," I replied, and my eyes drifted past him to the corridor beyond. Patrols. Crates. People moving too fast. "Things changed a little, didn't they."

Lee let out a dry breath that almost passed for a laugh. "That's for sure. My workload tripled. This is the first time my eyes have left a screen in forty eight hours." He rubbed his face with the heel of his hand, as if he could wipe the exhaustion away.

It hit me harder than it should have. Lee looked hollowed out. The light that used to live behind his jokes was dim, like someone had lowered it without asking. The man who was always quick with a remark now carried himself like every word cost him.

The war preparations were getting to him, too.

"Where's Raza," I asked, then added, almost as an afterthought, "and Michael?"

Lee's mouth tightened. "Working. Like crazy." He glanced down the corridor, already half leaving. "They split us across departments. Drilling, containment, routing. We're designing while the bores are already in the ground. Building as we go." His voice sharpened, not angry exactly, but worn raw. "Things get messy when you work like this. The leaders come up with a grand plan and expect us to perform magic overnight."

He shook his head once, slow.

The words landed in me like a delayed strike.

Because a lot of those "grand plans" had been mine. Ideas tossed onto a table with certainty, spoken like commands instead of burdens. I had pictured drills and corridors and clever traps as if they were lines on a map that could appear by will alone.

I had not pictured Lee's hands shaking from lack of sleep.

I had not pictured Raza and Michael swallowed by separate halls, separated not by distance, but by necessity.

War did not just take bodies. It took time. It took rest. It took the small bonds that made people human, and it spent them like coins.

My friends, who had only just become my friends, were being pulled apart by the very survival I insisted we needed. I should've pushed harder in that war room. I should've refused to feed their appetite for a physical battle.

And I had no title. No official authority.

Yet somehow I had become a lever that moved the whole city, and everyone beneath it paid the cost.

Lee forced a tired smile that didn't reach his eyes. "But it's good seeing you," he said. "Really. I just… I have to run."

He started to turn away.

"Lee," I said, and the word came out sharper than I meant, like I was trying to catch him before he disappeared into the machinery.

He paused, just barely, looking back.

I wasn't sure yet what I could offer him. An apology felt small. Gratitude felt useless.

But I couldn't let him walk away carrying all of it alone, but everyone is carrying a piece of the weight of Ashen Gate.

Chapter Twenty-Seven

REASSESS

2 days before the attack. The War Room.

"We're seventy-five percent complete on the drilling and burial works," the construction officer said. "But we're slipping behind schedule. The closer we get to completion, the slower everything becomes. The cuts have to be finer. The tolerances tighter." He tapped the display. "We're monitoring seismic activity in real time and pulling fresh core samples every hour to confirm the seabed can take the stress."

Ashcroft's gaze shifted down the table.

"Marshal Kade," he said. "Status."

Marshal Kade sat forward, shoulders squared, voice clipped and professional. "Troops are on continuous patrol throughout the city. We're escorting construction crews, reinforcing critical corridors, and rotating guard stations in the access arteries." She paused a fraction. "We're already starting to stretch thin."

Ashcroft did not react, but his eyes sharpened.

"There's been an uptick in violence across the residential sectors," Kade continued. "We've declared an internal state of emergency and we're supporting Civic Security where we can."

"Prefect Thomas," Ashcroft said, calm as stone.

Across the table, the Prefect Thomas tightened, hesitated, then spoke. It looked like he'd been carrying the words for a while.

"Yes, sir. It's escalating." He slid a report forward. "Arrests are up fifty percent. The pattern is consistent: shortages drive panic, panic drives crime. Robbery. Assault. Looting." His eyes flicked briefly to the others. "And it's not only desperation. It's suspicion. Neighbors turning on neighbors."

The room fell quiet in the way it did when everyone heard the same ugly truth at once.

Ashcroft's fingers rested on the table, motionless. Then he lifted his gaze and moved down the line of officials.

"Supply Director Jinsen."

Jinsen straightened, already looking worn thin.

"Getting supplies through Ashen Gate has become increasingly difficult," he said. "Farming and food processing have slowed drastically due to sudden labor shortages. People are calling out. Some simply aren't showing up at all."

He swallowed and continued.

"Deliveries are delayed by expanded checkpoints and security screenings. At the same time, demand has surged. Panic buying. Hoarding. Medical supplies are being pulled faster than we can replace them."

A pause and a breath.

"If current trends continue," Jinsen added carefully, "we will need to implement stricter rationing within days, not weeks."

Ashcroft remained silent for a long moment.

His fingers rested flat against the table, unmoving. He did not nod. He did not frown. If the report unsettled him, he did not allow it to show.

"Understood," he said at last.

Just that.

His eyes shifted briefly to the projected figures, then back to the officials seated around the table. Not alarmed. Not dismissive. Simply absorbing.

He leaned back slightly in his chair.

"We will address supply stability after the next status update," he added. "For now, keep distribution moving. Prioritize essentials. Maintain order."

No mention of panic.

No mention of morale.

No acknowledgment that something fragile was already bending.

To anyone watching, it looked like control.

To anyone listening closely, it sounded like a man choosing not to look too hard at a shadow he wasn't ready to name.

Each report hit me like a charge read aloud. The weight of what I'd caused settled on my shoulders.

If I had listened to Elit. If I had left the crew on Pilgrim's Wake and stuck to the mission, Ashen Gate might still be hidden and whole. Instead, it was bleeding from the inside out.

The meeting broke. Chairs scraped. Screens dimmed. Officials filed out, voices fading into the corridor.

I stayed.

Ashcroft stayed too, staring at the map like he could hold it together by will alone.

"General," I said quietly. "I've seen this before. If morale doesn't improve, we will lose the war."

Ashcroft didn't look up.

"I believe we already have," he said. "And it's my fault."

The words sounded practiced, as if he had been repeating them to himself for days.

"Pilgrim's Wake was my idea," he continued. "I commissioned the ship. I outlined the strike. I authorized the propaganda. I fed the city what it needed to hear so it would agree to what it feared."

He paused.

"Hensley was one of my best captains. I chose him myself to be captain of Pilgrim's Wake and lead the mission. He refused at first." Ashcroft's eyes finally flicked up, not to me, but to the map, as if it could contradict him. "But I pushed. I told him it was our people we were rescuing."

A pause in silence.

"Then new intelligence came in. It said we were under-armed. That the route was compromised. That if we launched, we would be guiding the Order straight back to our gate."

His hand shifted on the stone table, the smallest tremor in his fingers before he stilled them.

"So I called it off."

He exhaled slowly.

"But Hensley still believed he could do it," Ashcroft said. "He believed the risk was worth the souls in those jars. So he took the ship anyway. He stole it. Against my orders."

Ashcroft looked into the distance, shaking his head.

"And he riled up the crew and fired up a whole band of fighters. It was a mutiny. He used my own words to gather the troops. I could have stopped them, but the expense was too great."

He swallowed.

"The expense would be to lose control of Ashen Gate. Though I have the title, Hensley had the hearts of the people."

A bitter breath left him, almost a laugh, but there was no humor in it.

"And to my surprise… at the end of it all… they pulled it off. They retrieved the brains and slipped away clean."

His voice tightened, not with grief, but with the strain of forcing the truth through his teeth.

"Then the unexpected happened."

Ashcroft's gaze fixed on the table as if he could see the route laid out there, every turn, every mistake.

"The Reptilians intercepted them," he said. "Not like raiders."

A pause.

"Like allies who had come to help the Order."

"They slaughtered the troops without mercy," he said. "As if to extinguish our people. Everyone on board was a pilot or an engineer. They were not prepared to handle close-range combat."

He fell silent.

When he spoke again, it was quieter.

"I built Pilgrim's Wake to save our people," he said. "And instead I built the match that lit this war."

"We can do something about this," I said, the words coming faster now, urgency cutting through the fatigue. "But we have to restore morale before fear finishes the work the enemy hasn't even started."

Ashcroft finally looked at me. Not as a general. As a man running out of ground.

"What do you suggest?" he asked. No posturing. No rank in his voice. "I'm out of options."

I drew a breath, not because I needed it, but because the memory demanded it.

"When I was a private in the Continental Army, I didn't enlist because I wanted glory," I said. "I enlisted because it felt unavoidable. We were farmers, tradesmen, sons. Neighbors. We formed local militias because the alternative was to wait quietly for things to be decided for us."

I met his eyes.

"Then those militias were absorbed into the Continental Army. Suddenly, we weren't just defending a fence line or a road. We were part of something larger. Something shared."

I paused, choosing the words carefully.

"We believed we were freeing our land for a future we might never see. That our suffering meant our children wouldn't have to endure the same. We didn't think of ourselves as victims. We thought of ourselves as participants. Contributors."

Ashcroft remained silent, listening.

"Right now," I continued, "the people of Ashen Gate don't feel included. They feel managed. They feel watched. All they see are armed patrols and sealed corridors. Soldiers everywhere. Orders everywhere."

I gestured vaguely, toward the city above us.

"To them, it doesn't feel like protection. It feels like occupation."

His face tightened, but he didn't interrupt.

"They don't need more secrecy and a leader who says things are fine," I said. "They need purpose. They need to know why they're enduring this. They need to feel like Ashen Gate isn't something being defended over their heads, but something they are actively defending."

I leaned forward.

"They need to see you. Not as a commander behind stone walls, but as the face of this city. Speaking to them. Standing with them. Reminding them that this isn't about survival alone."

I let the final words land.

"It's about what kind of world survives."

For the first time in a long while, Ashcroft didn't look like a man carrying the city alone.

He looked like someone remembering why he picked it up in the first place.

Chapter Twenty-Eight

Speech

The day before the attack.

General Ashcroft took to the streets.

By then, the streets were almost unrecognizable. Garbage collection had stopped. Markets were shuttered behind metal slats. Lights that once felt warm now made everything look exposed. People either hid behind sealed doors or poured into the main concourse in angry waves.

It wasn't one crowd. It was three, braided together by fear.

Some held signs painted in clean block letters: NO WAR. ONLY PEACE.

Others carried rougher boards, splintered at the edges: DEATH TO THE ORDER.

And then there were the ones that made my stomach tighten: WE STAND FOR THE ORDER.

That last group was smaller, but they stood with an unsettling calm, as if they had already decided who would win and wanted to be forgiven early.

Voices collided from every angle. Arguments broke out and ended in shoves. Parents pulled children closer. Old men shouted scripture. Young men shouted back. Everyone spoke at once, not to be understood, but to drown out the terror underneath their words.

This was not the city I had arrived at.

Ashcroft stepped onto a raised platform at the center of the concourse. No armored wall. No barricade. Just him, a few feet of stone, and a sea of faces that looked ready to tear him apart.

It did not feel like he was about to give a speech.

It felt like a public execution.

He stood still while the noise hit him. He waited through the curses and the laughter and the names they threw like rocks.

I found myself holding my breath, though I didn't need air.

Ashcroft lifted one hand. Not a command. A gesture of patience.

The crowd did not quiet. Not fully. But the nearest people slowed their shouting, curious despite themselves.

He leaned toward the microphone. When he spoke, his voice was low and human, not booming. He did not reach for power. He reached for honesty.

"People of Ashen Gate," he began. "I won't insult you by pretending this is normal."

A few laughs snapped out, bitter.

He nodded once, like he accepted them.

"We are preparing for war."

The words didn't inflame the crowd. They sharpened it. Like a blade turned in the light.

Somewhere near the front, a woman screamed, "You brought war here!"

Another voice shouted, "We should surrender before we all die!"

A cluster to the left answered with a roar: "Never!"

Then came the booing, loud and ugly, rolling forward like a tide.

Ashcroft didn't flinch.

He let it crash.

He waited until the wave thinned enough for his next words to slip through.

"I hear you," he said. "All of you."

Someone hurled something small. It shattered on the stone near the stage. A glass bottle.

Ashcroft didn't even look down.

He looked into the crowd, directly, like he could pick out individual souls from the mass.

"I know what you're afraid of," he continued. "Because I am afraid too."

"Step down, resign!" yelled a man in the front.

Ashcroft's face tightened once, not in anger, but in restraint.

"They want us divided," he said. "Not because division is accidental. Because it is efficient."

He motioned subtly, not pointing at any one group, but acknowledging all of them.

"They don't need to break our walls if they can break our spirit. They don't need to breach the city if they can make the city breach itself."

A low murmur moved through the protestors like wind through dry grass.

"We have people here demanding peace," he said. "And you are not cowards. You are tired. You are protecting your children the only way you know how."

He turned slightly.

"We have people here demanding blood," he said. "And you are not monsters. You are furious because you know what the Order does to bodies. To choice. To freedom."

Then, carefully, he faced the third group.

"And we have people here saying we should stand for the Order," he said, voice steady. "Not because you love them. But because fear makes surrender look like safety."

That was the first time the Order-supporters shifted, the first time their calm cracked.

Ashcroft leaned closer to the microphone.

"I'm here to keep Ashen Gate from turning on itself."

The crowd churned again, but the tone changed. More listening. Even the angry ones wanted to hear what he'd say next, because he was still standing there, letting them hate him to his face.

He inhaled slowly.

"Tomorrow, they may come," Ashcroft said. "Or…they may choose something worse than soldiers. Silence. Fear. Psychological warfare."

"You're not even sure if they are coming?" Shouted a member of the crowd. A bustle of voices turned to thunder.

A pause.

"But there is one attack I know for certain is coming. The one that has already started."

He spread his hands.

"They want you to believe your neighbor is the enemy. They want you to believe the person beside you is either a fool, or a traitor, or a threat."

His voice hardened, just enough to hold the room.

"If that happens, we lose before the first shot is fired."

Somewhere, a child began to cry. A mother shushed them with shaking hands.

Ashcroft's tone softened again.

"I can't promise you a painless tomorrow," he said. "I can promise you this: if we face it together, we remain Ashen Gate. If we face it divided, we become victims to ourselves."

He stood taller.

"So here is what I ask of you. Not courage. Not heroics."

"Discipline."

"You cause a war and you want *us* to sacrifice?" a man in the crowd roared.

"Discipline to stop spreading rumors you can't prove," he said. "Discipline to share what you have instead of hoarding it like you're already dead. Discipline to keep your hands off your neighbor's throat."

A shout rose: "And what about you? What about your mistakes?"

Ashcroft didn't dodge.

He nodded once.

"You're right," he said. "I've made mistakes."

The crowd hissed, hungry for confession.

"I will answer for them," he said. "But I will not let the Order use them as a rope to strangle this city."

He lifted his chin.

"If you want to call me a fool, do it," he said. "If you want to curse me, do it. If you want to blame me, fine."

Then, quieter, deadly sincere:

"But do not make your children pay for it."

That line cut through the noise.

"They already *are* paying for it! You're sending them to war!"

"My son was sent on Pilgrim's Wake and never returned!"

That line fueled the crowd, and the crowd went wild. A riot exploded.

Ashcroft steadied his hands on the podium, as if anchoring himself to the stone.

Behind the stage, I realized my fists had clenched without me noticing.

Not from rage.

From fear.

Because for the first time, I understood the power of the Order's plan.

They didn't need to break the gate.

They just needed us to open it from the inside.

The first armored line of men moved in quickly. They stood between him and the crowd and formed a human shield.

Not fast. Not charging. Just a subtle tightening near the stage. A shift in posture. Hands closer to weapons. Shields angling forward.

The crowd noticed immediately.

Someone shouted, "Look! He brought soldiers to silence us!"

That was all it took.

The noise spiked, raw and panicked now. People surged toward the platform, not as one body but as a hundred conflicting impulses colliding at once. Fear ran faster than reason.

Ashcroft saw it too.

He raised both hands, palms open, trying to slow what he had accidentally set in motion.

"Wait," he said. "No...stand down. This is not what I..."

A sharp crack rang out as something struck the edge of the stage. Not aimed at him. Close enough to make the point.

That was when the security commander made the call.

Two guards stepped onto the platform, one on each side of Ashcroft. Not rough. Not apologetic either. Professional. Final.

"General," one said quietly, close enough that only Ashcroft could hear. "We have to move you. Now."

Ashcroft stiffened.

"I'm not finished," he said, low but firm.

Below, the front ranks were pressing forward hard enough that people stumbled. Someone fell. Others tripped over them. The sound of panic changed pitch.

The commander leaned in closer. "Sir, with respect, if you stay, they'll tear this place apart trying to reach you."

Ashcroft looked out over the crowd one last time.

For a heartbeat, he didn't look like a leader.

He looked like a man realizing he had lost the moment he was trying to save.

"All of you," he began, voice raised, desperate now. "Listen to me…"

A bottle shattered against the stone near his feet.

The guards didn't wait anymore.

They took his arms, not dragging him, but guiding him firmly toward the rear of the stage as a security wall surged up between the platform and the crowd.

The sight hit the people like confirmation.

"He's running!"

"They're silencing him!"

"See? See what power does!"

The shouting turned ugly.

Ashcroft twisted once, pulling against the guards just long enough to look back at the city.

"I am not abandoning you," he shouted over the noise. "Do not let fear turn you into weapons for someone else!"

But his words were swallowed whole.

The stage disappeared behind raised shields and bodies. Sirens began to pulse, low and controlled, trying to impose order where none remained.

I stood frozen at the edge of the concourse, watching the city tear at itself.

Not with guns.

Not with bombs.

With suspicion.

With blame.

With the terrible, human need to feel safe at any cost.

That was when it settled fully into my bones. The Order didn't need to attack. They were already winning.

They had turned Ashen Gate inward. And no wall in the world could stop that.

Bam.

A glass bottle shattered over my head.

I turned with a fit of rage, but caught myself.

"Clanker, get the hell out of here. You were made by the Order."

"How do we know you're not with them?"

"Or a spy?"

Smash.

Another bottle struck me

The world moved in slow motion as I made my way over to where General Ashcroft was dragged off to. I pushed my way through the crowd, that was beginning to turn on me.

Faces were violent, authority weakened, the streets weren't safe.

I jogged up the capital steps leaping over trash. Across the door was painted in dripping red paint, SURRENDER.

The keypad scanned my face. A soft chime. The doors swung inward.

I slipped through and they slammed shut behind me.

Inside was quiet. Not peaceful. Just muffled. The kind of quiet that comes after a scream when your ears are still ringing.

For one second, I stood still and let the silence hit me like relief.

Then I moved.

Fast.

The capital corridors were wide and clean, but the building felt hollow now, as if everyone with sense had already fled. My footsteps echoed loudly. My armor sounded like a weapon.

I turned a corner toward Ashcroft's wing.

And the emptiness ended.

A knot of officers, security, and staff had gathered at the far end of the hall. Their bodies were tight, shoulders rigid, faces pale in the sterile light. Someone was crying without making sound. Someone else stared forward like they'd been unplugged.

The air was still.

I slowed, not by choice. By instinct.

Words surfaced from the cluster, jagged and unreal.

"Ashcroft is dead!"

My body moved before my mind could accept it.

I ran towards his office.

Security snapped into motion, arms out, blocking me, hands on my chest plate.

"Stop!"

I shoved past just enough to see.

Over shoulders and heads, through the open office doorway, there was a shape on the floor.

General Ashcroft lay facedown in a dark pool of blood that spread across the stone floor like spilled ink.

His hand still held his sidearm covered in his own blood.

The gun looked small beside the weight of what it had done.

The room tilted.

My mind reached for the simplest answer and found none that didn't rot in my mouth.

Because if the Order didn't need to breach the city…

If they didn't need to fire a single shell…

Then this was the attack.

They had learned the shape of a human mind so well they could tilt an entire city with a whisper and watch it topple itself. Was mankind truly that naïve? Or were we simply predictable. Fragile in the places we pretended were strength.

Most of the turmoil in the streets had nothing to do with strategy. It was hunger. Exhaustion. Fear. People wanted comfort. People needed medicine. The Human of Flesh listened to their bodies, and their bodies steered the mind like reins. But the Order was mind alone, unburdened by flesh, unbothered by pain, untouched by the slow poisons that turn neighbors into enemies.

The Order had control because their people were content. Not happy, not alive the way we meant it, but regulated. They did not hunger. They did not lose sleep. Children were not born and raised, but produced and sorted, moved through a system like parts on a belt.

Had the Order truly eliminated unrest?

Or had they simply erased the conditions that create it?

And if so, did they do it because they were tyrants…

Or because they had already lived through what Ashen Gate was living now, and decided they would never endure it again?

That thought slid under my armor like cold water.

Their greatest threat was not us. It was the Reptilians and the Gray's. Strong forces. For the Order to survive at all, they would have had to evolve. Adapt. Harden. Not to enslave, I told myself, but to protect. To become something unbreakable in a universe that breaks everything.

So were we wrong the whole time?

Or were they simply right for themselves, and lethal to everyone else?

Nature did not apologize for transformation. A hermit crab outgrew its shell and stole another. A caterpillar surrendered its body to a chrysalis and woke as a different creature. A snake split itself open and slid free of what could no longer contain it.

Maybe that was all the Order claimed to be. A species shedding its skin.

But there was a difference between change and theft. Between choosing a new shell and being ripped from your own.

Humans progressed as a whole by invisible hands. Empires rose. Faiths fractured. Men marched because other men told them it was destiny. Society moved like a tide, and every man inside it called the current "history" to feel less helpless.

Maybe that was the trap.

Maybe destiny was just a word we used when we were afraid to admit we could have chosen differently.

Like chasing a whale with a harpoon, swearing you were hunting evil, until the rope caught your foot and the sea took you in.

Down into the depths we all fell, not because the ocean wanted us…

But because we would not let go.

Chapter Twenty-Nine

Return

Something inside me shifted. The world looked different now, not because Elit had spoken, but because his words had landed somewhere deeper than trust.

It was no longer a question of whether I trusted him.

It was whether I trusted any system at all.

Today was supposed to be the day of the Order's attack. The day we had prepared for. The day we had ruined ourselves trying to survive.

But Ashen Gate was already in pieces.

Ashcroft was gone. Marshal Kade had taken his place, but what she inherited was not a command, it was a wreck. A city held together by emergency protocols and exhausted hands. A chain of authority that still existed on paper even as it frayed in real time.

We monitored above the water anyway. Every sensor. Every listening post. Every scope and screen.

Nothing.

No ships. No insertion shells. No tremor in the sea.

Just absence.

And absence, I was learning, could be louder than any alarm.

At the round table, officials spoke in tired loops. Numbers. Coverage zones. Patrol rotations. Food. Arrests. Rumors. The same words, reshuffled like desperate prayers.

I listened until I couldn't.

Then I stood.

"I'm going above the water."

A few heads snapped up. A few eyes narrowed, not in anger, but in fear. Fear of what my decision might mean. Fear of what it might trigger.

Marshal Kade's posture tightened like she was bracing for impact.

"We'll notify Calder, your co-pilot," she offered, quick and automatic, already reaching for procedure like it could hold the day together.

"No need," I said.

"I'm going alone."

The room went still. Even the screens seemed to dim, as if the city itself paused to listen.

Kade pushed back from the table, half rising.

"Gregory, if this is a trap…"

"If it's a trap," I cut in, "then it's already sprung. We're just waiting here to feel it close."

My gaze moved around the table. Around the worn faces. The brittle patience. The fear disguised as planning.

"We built shafts to swallow shells that never came," I said quietly. "We turned our streets into checkpoints. We turned neighbors into suspects. If the Order wanted us to collapse, we helped them."

Kade held my eyes.

"You don't have authority," someone muttered. A council voice. A relic of the old order, clinging to titles like life preservers.

I almost laughed.

Authority.

Ashcroft's empty chair sat at the head like a grave marker.

I turned toward the door.

Behind me, Kade's voice followed, controlled but strained.

"If you leave the city right now, and you're intercepted, we may not get you back."

I paused at the threshold, hand on the seam where the door would split.

"I know," I said.

Then, softer, more honest than I meant it to be:

"But I can't sit here and pretend nothing is wrong just because the sky is quiet."

I stepped through.

The door sealed behind me with a hiss that sounded too much like a last breath.

I walked toward the exit, and two guards met me at the doors like they'd been waiting for a shift change.

One of them glanced past my shoulder, then back at me.

"It's getting bad out there," he said, the way a man comments on rain. "Be careful."

I nodded once.

The doors split with a hiss.

Noise hit me first. Not a single sound, but layers of it. Shouting. Metal scraping. Footsteps slamming stone. A crowd so thick it seemed to have its own gravity.

It was larger than before. Larger by far.

And the moment they saw me, it moved as one body.

Barricades toppled like toys. People shoved through gaps, vaulted railings, spilled over fences with the same frantic purpose. Not to listen. Not to argue.

To hurt.

The charging crowd swallowed me whole.

I braced and raised my arms, covering my face more out of instinct than need.

They struck me and knocked me to the ground. I rolled up into the fetal position.

Hands grabbed my armor and yanked. Knuckles hammered metal. Boots thudded into my ribs and back. Someone swung something hard that rang off my shoulder plate like a bell. Under the sheer weight of a stampeding crowd, I felt my body crumple.

Bodies piled. Hot breath. Rage in a hundred throats.

The guards tried to hold them back. I heard the sharp pop of gas canisters. Saw brief flashes of electric restraint devices. Heard commands shouted and swallowed.

Nothing held.

Nothing slowed the fury.

My vision stuttered in waves, brightness dimming and returning, like a failing lamp.

I felt something in me crack.

Not the armor.

Something deeper.

RAGE.

ENOUGH!

I pushed my palms into the stone and forced myself upright. The mass around me slid, stumbled, reeled back as if the ground had suddenly tilted.

My head lifted.

Faces stared up at me from inches away. Spit-flecked. Wide-eyed. Furious. Afraid.

And I hated what I saw when I looked at them.

Human of Flesh are ANIMALS, vicious and vile.

It was Elit's voice.

Or mine.

I swung my fists with rage and raw panic with all my strength. My arm cut through the air and bodies. A man went down hard. Another caught the edge of my forearm plate and flew backward into the crowd.

Someone screamed.

The scream did something to me. It wasn't fear. It was the sound of consequence.

I stopped just long enough to see what I'd done.

Not enemies.

People.

Hungry people. Terrified people. People whose city had been turned inside out.

And still they came.

That was the worst part. Not their anger.

Their desperation.

They surged again, clawing at me like I was the shape of everything they couldn't control. Hands on my throat. Hands on my helmet seam. Hands trying to pry me open and prove I bleed like they did.

I shoved forward, forcing a path with my shoulders, with my weight, with the brutal certainty of metal moving through flesh.

"Get back!" I shouted, but it came out wrong. It came out like a threat, not a warning.

My suit was smeared dark. Not just dust and grime anymore.

Blood.

I saw it on my forearm, in the joints of my plating, in the shine of my chest light. I saw it and felt nothing.

That terrified me, but the fear was fleeting.

Then the crowd parted for a fraction of a second, and through the gap, I caught a glimpse of her.

Raza.

At the edge of the chaos, half-hidden behind bodies. Her face drawn tight, eyes locked on me. Not angry.

Horrified.

Like she was watching someone she knew disappear.

I should have felt something then. A pull. A stab. Anything.

But the place inside me that held warmth had gone quiet.

I turned away before it could wake.

The mob was breaking now, not because it had calmed, but because fear had finally found a shape. They were backing up, tripping over each other, dragging the wounded, shouting warnings instead of accusations.

I stood there in the churn of it, breathing for no reason, staring at what I'd become in a matter of seconds.

A monster.

Too far gone.

I broke into a run.

Not away from them.

Away from myself.

I sprinted for the hangar, boots clanging, shoulders cutting through fleeing bodies and scattered debris. The air smelled like gas and sweat. I vaulted a fallen barrier, hit the hangar threshold, and didn't slow.

The Piercer waited in its bay like a knife in a sheath.

I climbed the ladder in two pulls, dropped into the cockpit, and slapped the canopy seal.

The world outside became muffled. Distant. Like a memory.

My hands found the yoke and throttle without thought.

The engines answered.

The Piercer surged forward.

I left Ashen Gate behind me without ceremony.

The city receded into darkness beneath the ocean, its lights flickering like a constellation drowning in stone. A place built to last. A place already cracking from the inside.

I should have felt guilt.

I felt clarity.

The Order had not come. Not with ships. Not with soldiers. Not with shells.

They didn't need to.

Ashen Gate was already at war with itself.

I thought of the riots. The hunger. The fear that spread faster than any weapon. I thought of how easily people turned when their bodies were pushed past their limits.

Then I thought of my own stillness.

No hunger.

No exhaustion.

No pain clouding judgment.

Only thought.

Only intent.

The Piercer climbed, breaking the surface, rising into open sky. For a moment, suspended between water and air, flesh and metal, past and future, I understood the terrible simplicity of it all.

Humanity had not been conquered.

It had been outgrown.

And whether that evolution was salvation or extinction depended on a question I no longer knew how to answer:

Was suffering proof of life?

Or proof that life needed to change?

I didn't turn back.

Not because I had chosen the Order.

But because I was no longer certain Ashen Gate could survive the truth.

Ashen Gate had walls thick enough to stop armies.

It still collapsed.

Not from weapons.

From fear.

Hunger.

Pain.

I looked down at my hands.

The stains of blood.

If this is what it means to be human…

Then perhaps humanity has reached the end of what flesh can carry.

Gregory's story continues…

Printed in Dunstable, United Kingdom

79231139R00190